Praise for *A Fostered Love* by Cameron Dane

"Cameron Dane's fans won't be disappointed and those new to her writing will add her to their list of favorites."

— *Literary Nymphs*

"The writing is first-rate. Character histories and passions are beautifully revealed in ways that feel natural and coherent rather than contrived and artificial."

— Matthew, *Rainbow Reviews*

"*A Fostered Love* has angst, love, and hot man love to keep you turning the pages and wanting more of Cameron Dane in the future."

— Tina, *Two Lips Reviews*

A Recommended Read! "I have yet to read a book by Cameron Dane that has failed to keep me so deeply engrossed that I lose track of time. I eagerly await each and every offering from this fantastic author."

— Hayley, *Fallen Angel Reviews*

"Cameron Dane can write great romances and *A Fostered Love* is one of her best."

— April, *The Romance Studio*

D0109781

Loose Id®

ISBN 13: 978-1-60737-401-5
A FOSTERED LOVE
Copyright © September 2009 by Cameron Dane
Originally released in e-book format in March 2009

Cover Art by Anne Cain
Cover Layout and Design by April Martinez

DISCLAIMER: Many of the acts described in our BDSM/fetish titles can be dangerous. Please do not try any new sexual practice, whether it be fire, rope, or whip play, without the guidance of an experienced practitioner. Neither Loose Id nor its authors will be responsible for any loss, harm, injury or death resulting from use of the information contained in any of its titles.

This book is an original publication of Loose Id. Each individual story herein was previously published in e-book format only by Loose Id and is a work of fiction. Any similarity to actual persons, events or existing locations is entirely coincidental.

Printed in the U.S.A. by
Lightning Source, Inc.
1246 Heil Quaker Blvd
La Vergne TN 37086
www.lightningsource.com

A FOSTERED LOVE

Dedication

To Dad, for fostering my love of reading. I can still remember the first time my dad put a "big people" book in my hand and said, "Try reading it to yourself. If you have some trouble, come to me, and I'll help you figure it out." I never looked back. Thanks for always caving in and letting me buy more than one book when we went to the bookstore. – CD

Prologue

Holy shit, it's him.

Jonah Roberts, all grown up.

Christian opened his mouth, but nothing came out. He stared through the screen door at the man waiting on the other side, and Christian regressed fifteen years, to when, standing in this very spot, his world shattered as the cops took Jonah away. Jonah had been sixteen, and Christian a wiry fourteen-year-old kid, scared to death.

Christian never thought to see his old bunkmate again.

Only, here Jonah stood, all these years later, a man.

Jonah leaned in and braced his hand on the door frame, the motion popping the muscles under the snug fit of his T-shirt. Christian followed the line down to a flat stomach but took an automatic step back and dropped his gaze to the carpeted floor before it could travel any lower on Jonah Roberts's body.

A throat cleared—so sexy to Christian's ears—and he snapped his attention back up to Jonah. The rough edges mapping the face on the other side of the screen hardened, and a hairline scar that cut across Jonah's brow—Christian remembered that imperfection well—stood out pale against his olive skin. Gray eyes that Christian swore to God were so pale they looked silver nailed Christian in place through the barrier of the door.

"A lawyer contacted me and told me Marisol wanted me to come," Jonah said. Christian's chest ached at the name, the loss still too fresh to examine. "I'll stay at a motel and won't get in the way of anything, but I wanted to come and pay my respects."

"I'm surprised the lawyer was able to find you." Old hurts surfaced, and Christian couldn't stuff them down where the twenty-eight-year-old man he was now knew they should stay. "Most of the people she fostered for as short a time as you just called on the phone or said they were sorry through the lawyer. And none of them told me Mari requested they come."

"I don't care about any of them," Jonah growled. "None of those fucking people are me, Christian."

Christian's heart still fluttered, all these years later. Jonah was the only one who didn't call him Chris, and for the three months they shared a home, Christian lived for when big, angry, teenage Jonah uttered his full name. "She wanted me here, so here I am. Are you going to let me into her home or not?"

Christian wanted to scream "No!" with every fiber of his being. *Not the scene of the crime, please. Why would you do this to me, Mari?*

"Yes, sorry." Christian unlatched the door, proud that his fingers remained steady. "Come on in."

Jonah grabbed the handle on the other side and pulled, and Christian quickly moved out of the way. Pausing as he stepped over the threshold, Jonah stood only inches from Christian, charging the air around him with unmistakable testosterone and vitality. Christian watched as Jonah took in the outdated living room before him. While Christian stood aside, he drank in Jonah's six-feet-three height, and he couldn't help measuring it against his own much-less-impressive five-eleven. Wide shoulders tapered down a back that Christian just knew was covered in ropes of muscle, ending with an ass that looked damn tight and fuckable, no matter that dark jeans shielded the cheeks and crease. Christian may not know much about men—God, how his life recently had proven that—but he could discreetly spot a nice butt with the best of them.

"Christ," Jonah uttered, his voice sounding in awe, "this place hasn't changed since the day I left."

Christian tried to view the converted double shotgun house through eyes that hadn't looked upon it every day from age twelve to eighteen, and then at least two or three times a week for the last five. The small living room had a dusky pink couch with a cabbage rose pattern, and the coffee table was made of cheap wood with spindle legs. Two overstuffed recliners—one blue, one green—had seen better days, and the wood paneling on the walls definitely darkened the room to almost cavelike when the green curtains on the front window were pulled closed. The dining room that sat one wall behind this room, and then the kitchen one wall farther back, held similarly dated designs.

Jonah started to walk with a purposeful stride down the single hallway, opening doors on the opposite side as he went. Christian stayed right on his heels. Jonah glanced in the direction of the dining room as he passed it, paused when he reached the bedroom he briefly shared with Christian, but shook his head and moved on. He continued to the back of the house, stopping at the screened back door. To the left lay the only bathroom in the home and to the right an open area that served as the laundry room. Jonah stopped at the back door and stared out to the yard beyond.

"The yard is in great shape," Jonah finally said, although he didn't turn around. "It has that going for it, at least."

"I did the best I could." Christian's hackles rose, and he gritted his teeth. "She didn't want the inside of the house redone."

Marisol Ramirez might not have adopted him, but from the day Christian met her, she had become his emotional rock. Christian for damn sure would not accept *this* man insinuating he had neglected her. "I did the upgrades she would allow, but I had no intention of forcing a more modern decor on her when she didn't want it."

"She may not have wanted it, but if you're gonna sell this home and make top dollar, you're gonna need to make some serious improvements." Jonah turned and leaned his shoulder against the doorjamb. He crossed his arms against his chest, revealing the bottom half of a tattoo on his upper arm. Jonah's next words tore Christian's gaze away from trying to figure out the design. "And you're gonna need some help."

Christian shook his head, the hairs on the back of his neck rising again. "You don't need to worry about that. I'm going to honor her wishes and do the very best I can."

"And I'm going to help you." Jonah went right on as if Christian hadn't even spoken. "I've changed my mind about the motel. Where should I put my bag? I'm gonna be staying awhile."

"Here?" Christian's voice came out tighter than he would have liked. He cleared his throat and set a hard stare on the big man—this *stranger*—in front of him. "In this house?"

"That's what I said." Jonah nodded.

No. Fucking. Way.

Chapter One

Jonah straightened his tie, grimacing as he fought the urge to rip it off his neck. He tore his gaze down from the bathroom mirror, hating the hardness in his face that made people look at him twice and then steer away from his path. Made them think he was an animal without any feelings too, which, in general, he didn't let bother him too much. It served him well in his line of work, and he'd never really cared enough about any one person to point out that he had no control over the face and body his good-for-nothing parents had given him.

He cared what Christian thought.

Jonah cared the damn kid could sense how much Jonah loved and valued Marisol Ramirez, even if she hadn't been able to keep him out of trouble. Jonah laughed and shook his head, taking another look at the cynical man in the mirror. "He's not such a kid anymore, Roberts. Stop trying to pretend you didn't notice it right away."

Damn thing was, Jonah didn't understand why he had taken notice of Christian's face and body. Years ago, when he seriously started thinking about sex, he had never given much consideration to being straight or gay or even bi. Jonah didn't emotionally connect to *anybody* and so simply relieved the urge to fuck where the opportunities presented themselves. That had consisted of a handful of women over the years, a guy who sucked his cock as a form of payment for fixing his Harley, and one other exchange of blowjobs with a neighbor, just because they'd both been horny. Other than that, fixing bikes and custom cars occupied most of Jonah's waking hours, and he didn't let the lack of a real connection in his life worry him.

For the most part anyway.

On those nights when sleep wouldn't come, Jonah often looked back on the time he spent in Marisol's home and the absolutely pushy kindness she showed him, no matter how big an attitude he threw her way. Then there was his roommate, inquisitive Christian…Jonah's shadow. Jonah thought about Christian during those darkest hours of the night and often let his mind wander to the man he must have become under Marisol's loving care.

In those moments, Jonah's cock stirred, and he fantasized about being able to connect with someone in a deeper, more real way than he had been able to achieve thus far. He thought about connecting with dark-eyed Christian, and what it would feel like to kiss him as a man.

Jonah's prick pushed against his dress pants, disgusting him. Christ, maybe he really didn't have any feelings in him at all. A woman was being buried today, for fuck's sake, and here he stood, getting a hard-on.

A sharp rap of knuckles hit the bathroom door. "Come on, man." Christian's smooth, deep voice reached through the wood and settled a shiver over Jonah. "I have to get going to the funeral home. So unless you want to ride your bike…"

Jonah growled at his reflection one last time. Running his hands down the expensive suit that felt so, so wrong on him, he turned in the small bathroom and whipped open the door. "No"—he white-knuckled the wood, his heart suddenly racing at what he would face today—"you know I don't want to arrive on my bike. I don't want to disrespect Marisol like that."

Some of the visible tightness left Christian's body, and his stance relaxed. Jonah tried not to notice how handsome Christian looked in his tan suit and pale blue tie. "You know she wouldn't care about that, Jonah."

"Maybe not." Jonah's words came across as a censure or a command, but he had long ago given up trying to figure out how to soften his voice. It sounded like bricks in a cement mixer, and there wasn't a damn thing he could do to change it. "But I would."

Christian's lips blanched and narrowed to a thin line. "Right. If you're ready"—he glanced toward the front of the house—"we really need to go."

Jesus, Jonah had never formally mourned a person's passing before. "Guess we can't put it off any longer." He pushed past Christian, suddenly uncomfortable with having the man see him. Clenching his fists as he walked through the small house to Christian's truck, Jonah psyched himself up for the spectacle of a funeral.

* * *

Jonah stood a little back and to the left of Christian, confused as he watched people filling the church annex, mingling and going to the table of food as if they attended a party. He understood the *concept* of people gathering after the death of a family member or friend, but he didn't see how it actually helped the grieving process for those closest to the dead.

As he watched Christian shake the hand of person after person and say thank you a thousand times, it was clear to Jonah that the strain only grew in Christian, not the other way around. The younger man took no strength in hearing strangers say how much they loved Marisol—at least not right now. Maybe in a month or two or six, he would welcome stories about how many lives Marisol had changed for the better, but not today. Today, Christian barely looked like he was breathing.

Looking at Christian's back, a funny itching sensation tingled over Jonah's palms, making him want to touch Christian in some way; to offer comfort, even though he didn't have any idea how in the hell to do it. If these people who'd known Christian and Marisol for all these years couldn't ease Christian's pain, Jonah didn't see how in the hell he was supposed to do it. Still, Jonah moved in and reached out to rest his hand against the widest part of Christian's back—

"Jonah Roberts"—a female voice reached Jonah's ears, and he snatched his hand back—"is that you?"

This time, a hand touched *his* back, and Jonah stiffened at the contact before turning. A tall woman with flaming red hair, porcelain skin, and pure blue eyes stood in front of him. Familiarity whispered across Jonah's senses, but a name or a place eluded him. He couldn't think much beyond Christian standing some six feet away from him, as he heard another scratchy "thank you for your kindness" leave the man's lips.

"You have a unique face, and I would never forget it." Before Jonah could take offense or speak a word, the woman broke out into a smile and held out her hand. "But you don't have any idea who I am, do you?"

"Your eyes look familiar." Jonah slipped his hand into hers and got a good hard shake in response. "But a name or place isn't coming to me. Sorry." He'd gotten used to apologizing for things that he *thought* might hurt someone else's feelings, rather than feeling any true sense of regret for the slight. "I have my mind on other things today."

"Of course." She blinked fast a few times as she nodded. "Mari was the best. I'm Abby. I went into Mari's care maybe two or three weeks before you"—a blush stole over her face, flaming the pale skin red—"left."

"Before I was arrested, you mean." *Damn it.* Jonah wanted to steal back the words as soon as they left his mouth. That was not an appropriate thing to say at a funeral. Even he knew that much. "Sorry again." He studied the young woman and tried to peel back the layers of age. The picture of a small body scampering across the living room into a corner filled his mind. "Right. I remember you now. You liked to hide. You were eight, maybe?"

"Eleven, actually. Hadn't had my growth spurt yet. And yeah, that was me." She laughed, but Jonah thought it had a nervous quality to it. "I didn't last very long at Mari's"—right then, clouds washed across her eyes—"but hers was by far the best home out of all the places I lived. Christian was always very sweet to me, and we somehow managed to stay friends." Lifting on the tiptoes of her heels, she looked around Jonah's shoulder. Immediately, her brow furrowed. "I wanted to see how he was doing. I guess I missed him."

Jonah spun around and found the space next to Father Abel filled by another foster child of Marisol's. Christian had introduced the man as Rodrigo.

"*Shit.*" Jonah thought he'd kept the curse under his breath until Abby widened her eyes in his direction. "Sorry—for a third time." Jonah kicked himself for not watching more closely and missing Christian's escape. "Will you excuse me?" He didn't wait for her answer. He pumped her hand again quickly. "It was good to see you. Thanks."

Leaving Abby standing by herself, Jonah strode across the big hall, searching for the exits. He discarded the front double doors as too obvious and moved for the kitchenette instead. Jonah sidestepped small groups of mourners, none of whom seemed particularly mournful. Yet again, an understanding of these types of social situations—that as a thirty-one-year-old man should be old hat to him by now—eluded him. Fuck, Jonah just wanted to get the hell out of this place and start the updates to Marisol's home.

But not until I find Christian.

Jonah reached the kitchenette and, as expected, found a back door. Easing it open, Jonah scanned the small parking area and open lot beyond. Empty. He slumped his shoulder against the doorjamb, deflating as he accepted that he had incorrectly guessed Christian's whereabouts. Logically, it seemed so much less likely Christian would have gone out the front. He would have encountered more people who wanted to talk to him about Marisol, and it really seemed to

Jonah like Christian needed out of that grind of forced politeness for a while.

Right. Just goes to show how fucking little you know about anything that doesn't involve a motorcycle engine— particularly in regard to people, but most especially about Christian Sanchez.

Jonah shifted his weight off where he leaned and started to close the door. As he did, the scuffle of gravel and a furious whisper of voices reached his ears.

"I already told you"—that voice definitely belonged to Christian, and it sounded very tight-lipped to Jonah—"I don't need your help. I just want five minutes of peace away from everybody. That includes you."

"And I already told you I was sorry about how everything went down," the other voice, another man, said. "But that doesn't mean I don't care about you or want to help you during this time. God, man, you loved her. I know you're hurting."

Trapped, Jonah stayed stock-still, unsure what to do. A simmer bubbled just beneath the surface, one that urged him to show himself and grab Christian away from this other person. Clearly, Christian did not want this guy's help. On the other hand, if Jonah stepped out of the shadows, Christian might think he had been spying, and Jonah didn't want that. He could step back, but the door would creak and give him away. Maybe when it did, Jonah could pretend he was just popping outside for some fresh air.

"Whatever I am," Christian went on, "is no business of yours. Not anymore. Now leave me alone."

"I can't. I still want us—"

"Get"—a cutting edge took over Christian's voice—"your hands off me."

"Give me a chance."

"Let go." Ice. Christian was pure ice. "Now."

"No—"

Okay. No, the fuck, way.

"Excuse me." Jonah moved out of the shadows and quickly took in a blond man holding Christian by the upper arms. The guy was bigger than Christian, but nowhere near the size of Jonah. Heat at the picture Jonah witnessed hit him full force. "You need to get your hands the hell off Christian before I put a fist in your face."

Chapter Two

Jonah's hard-cutting tone, uttering, "Get your hands the hell off Christian," froze Christian in place. *Oh God.* His heart raced terribly, and his eyes slid closed. *Why? Why did he have to be the one to walk outside and see me like this?*

Apparently, fifteen years apart had done nothing to dim Christian's unique ability to humiliate himself in front of Jonah Roberts. *Damn it.* Christian had only wanted five minutes alone to pull himself together and prepare for the next wave of well-wishers. Only, what did he get? Followed by the one man he really could not deal with right now and then treated to a case of overprotection by the one guy who had haunted his dreams for too many years.

In that moment, Christian wanted to shove both of them aside and run the hell away.

"*Always be proud*, mijo," whispered in Christian's ear, jerking him out of his stupor. "*No one can make you feel inferior but you.*" Mari's words fluttered inside Christian, settling the pounding in his chest and the roaring in his ears.

"Jonah," Christian started.

"I'm waiting," Jonah said softly, as if he had not heard Christian speak his name. He never looked away from David, who still held Christian's arms in a strong grip. Jonah's pale, flat gaze pierced right through David, and the coldness made Christian shiver. "Unless you think you need some help unwrapping your fingers from Christian's arms, in which case..." Jonah made one menacing move forward, and that was all it took. David pulled his hands away and held them up in front of him for good measure.

Beside Christian, David said, "We were just talking."

"You were *handling*." Jonah corrected, his hands clenching into fists at his sides. "And you're bigger than he is, but I'm bigger than you." He reached them in three fast strides and leaned into David's space. "Does that mean I get to grab you and call it *talking?*"

Goddamnit, I don't need this shit today. "Okay, enough!" Christian's voice cracked across the air. He stepped in front of David, forcibly edging Jonah backward. Already exhausted, and knowing the day wasn't even close to over yet, Christian was in no mood to referee a pissing contest. "We buried a woman today, and I don't know about you two, but I tend to think that means this day *isn't about me.* So if the two of you don't back the fuck off and go to your own corners, I'm gonna wonder if either one of you really gives a shit about that. I came out here for five minutes of quiet, but I see now I was better off inside. Excuse me"—he shoved past Jonah and didn't bother to look back at David—"I need to get back inside."

Christian fumbled with the door and pushed his way into the annex, pausing in the kitchenette in order to get his bearings. *Jesus fucking Christ.* How many times was he going to have to tell David that he would not meet him in a motel room ever again before the guy stopped harassing him?

David had a wife now, yet he continued to corner Christian, pushing for a restart to their relationship. Christian usually found it irritating but easy to fend off. Today, David had crossed a line. David knew how much Marisol meant to Christian, and for him to show up at her funeral to try and get at Christian while his defenses were down went well beyond bad taste. He did not know what in the hell to do about David anymore.

Then there was Jonah. Damn it, why did he have to walk outside right then? One more minute and Christian would have handled David and had him on his way home to his wife, as he'd done a half dozen times since the calls and cornering had begun three months ago. Now Jonah, God, *Jonah*, would remember everything about Christian, would remember what Christian had so stupidly done that night Jonah was arrested.

"I'm sorry." Jonah's rough voice cut across the small kitchen, startling Christian…and licking at him like a prickly caress. "I shouldn't have intruded." Out of the corner of his eye, Christian caught Jonah standing in the doorway. "It wasn't my place."

Christian took a steadying breath and turned to face Jonah head-on. "I could have handled it." He stood his ground, steady as a rock. "I'm not the gawky fourteen-year-old kid you knew all those years ago."

Jonah didn't move, but his focus dropped down Christian's body, only to steadily work its way up to meet Christian's eyes again. "No, I can see that. You're a man."

Now why did that feel like nothing so much as a caress of his naked flesh? *Let go of your silly crush, Christian.*

Listen to your own words. You're an adult now. "It wasn't what you—"

"It's because of being in JD." The words suddenly burst from Jonah in a rush. "When you're locked up with kids who don't want to be your friend and never have a reason to touch you that isn't followed by a beat down, you don't let someone who grabs you hold on for more than one second. I saw that guy holding your arms, and in my head I thought you were going to be hurt." Jonah clenched his fists at his sides as red burned across the hard lines of his cheeks. "I didn't think. I just reacted. I'm sorry."

"Oh." Christian's stomach fluttered, even though he wished like hell it didn't. "Well…"

"I know you've never been in trouble like that"—Jonah suddenly shoved his hands into his pockets—"like I was. I needed to take a minute and think, and remind myself that you don't hang out with people who would fight."

Christian chuckled and raised a brow. "I don't know about that."

Somehow, Jonah's cheeks grew even ruddier. "Other than me, I mean."

Those words twisted right at Christian's heart. "I wasn't talking about you."

"Oh." Jonah didn't break the stare, and Christian took one step forward, pulled by a force that still held him as strongly as that starry-eyed kid with a crush. As Christian had told Jonah, though, he wasn't a boy anymore. He was a man.

But so was Jonah. And that man didn't look away from Christian's stare.

Breathing through a heart that raced too fast, Christian took another step closer to Jonah. Jonah made a move too.

"Hi, Chris." Abby popped into the kitchen right then, stalling both men in place, a half dozen feet still between them. Christian took a good look at how close he stood to Jonah, gave a clearheaded thought to what he would have done if they'd gotten any closer, and he silently thanked Abby for saving him from making a colossal fool of himself in front of Jonah. Again.

"Hi again." Abby flashed Jonah a fast smile but quickly turned to Christian. "It's good to see you. We'll talk later, but right now, I think you need to go rescue Rodrigo. He has a look in his eyes that makes me think he wants to bang some heads together."

"Right." Christian couldn't believe, even for one second, that he had lost himself in Jonah's pale gaze and forgotten where he was, and why he was here. *Have some respect for the woman who saved your life, asshole. Mari is dead, and people are here to honor the selfless life she lived.* "You could be right about Rodrigo." The older man had little patience for small talk and usually wasn't tactful enough to pretend otherwise. "Thank you."

"No problem." Abby gave a small smile and disappeared from the kitchenette as quickly as she had come.

Turning, Christian found Jonah those few feet away, his hand on the doorknob. "I have to get back," Christian said, hoping the heat burning his face didn't show under his coloring. "I'll find you when it's time to go, okay?"

"That's all right." Jonah pulled open the back door and braced his hand on the wood. "I'll walk back to the house. I guess I'm kind of like Rodrigo." He lifted his finger and made a little circling gesture. "I don't know how much more of this I can take."

Christian dipped his head. "I understand. I'll see you later then. We can talk about what we want to do to prepare the house for sale."

"Sounds good." Jonah offered a small wave. "Bye."

Christian went in one direction, and Jonah went in the other.

* * *

Jonah let himself into the house, grateful he'd gone ahead and bought enough food for two. Christian's truck now sat in the driveway, so the last of the well-wishers must have finally left the annex. When seven o'clock came and went, Jonah started to wonder if Christian would get home tonight at all. By eight, his stomach went well past grumbling to outright protesting, and he hopped on his bike to see what kind of place he might find open on a Sunday night.

All Jonah needed was a good burger joint, and he found the one he remembered enjoying, still in business and open till midnight. A sense of the surreal surrounded Jonah as he drove around Coleman, and he wondered how in the hell a town could look almost exactly as it had fifteen years ago. Florida had grown by leaps and bounds in the last decade, but certain sections of this place seemed trapped in time.

Sort of the way Marisol's house looks and feels, trapped in another decade.

That would have to change if Christian intended to honor the woman's final request. Marisol wanted Christian to sell the house for as much as he could possibly get and split the proceeds up among three children's charities she had supported and loved.

Steeling himself, Jonah muttered, "No time like the present to make a plan."

He tossed the bag of food on the coffee table and made his way through the house to the kitchen. "Christian," he called. "I have food. Come and get it!" He opened the fridge and, not seeing any beer, grabbed a couple cans of soda.

On his way back to the front room, Jonah started opening bedroom doors. He opened the third of four and stopped dead in his tracks. Christian lay fast asleep on one of the two beds. The other bed, where Jonah slept for such a brief time in his teen years, lay empty, neat and made, with the same blue plaid blanket he remembered covering it some fifteen years ago.

Jonah didn't have the ability to reminisce or focus on his old bed right now. His gaze stayed glued on Christian, and more importantly, on his dark tan back, bare and beautiful, in the shadows.

Shit.

Jonah's cock stirred, and that shocked him almost as much as anything else these last few days. Not that he could sport half wood for Christian, or even just another man, but that it happened with so little effort. Jonah could get it up for the task of fucking, but it usually required a couple of good hard strokes of his dick, whether by hand or mouth. He also usually had to do a fair bit of touching the other person's body before he really got into it enough to not only have sex, but simply to *want* to have sex.

Not right now.

Jesus, he could pull Christian's pants down just enough to get at his tight ass and take him right here, no foreplay or other handling required. He could press his weight into Christian's back and stick his face in the guy's dark, silky-looking hair, and fuck him for half the damn night. Hell, maybe all night. His pecker was still young enough to do it.

Jonah made a move without even realizing he did it, and stepped right on a pile of clothes. Looking down, he found Christian's jacket, tie, shirt, and shoes, and that made Jonah's stomach twist up all funny. *He's so exhausted.* More than just information to process, it pushed at Jonah enough that he bent down and picked up the clothes, straightening them before laying them out across his old bed.

That done, Jonah closed the door softly and left Christian to some much-needed sleep. His food forgotten, Jonah searched for Marisol's address book and made some calls.

* * *

Ding-dong. Ding-dong.

The two-beat gong of the ancient doorbell sounded through the small house, jerking Christian out of sleep. He rolled toward his familiar alarm clock and almost fell right out of bed. Cursing the low bed he hadn't slept in since he was eighteen years old, he shot his hand out and braced it against the threadbare carpet, righting himself before he cracked his head into the bookshelf that butted up against the wall between the two single beds.

Ding-dong. Ding-dong.

Son of a bitch, the person was damn impatient. "Give me a second to get out of bed, for God's sake." He scrubbed his face with his hands as he treaded out of the bedroom on bare feet. Yawning, he slapped his cheeks to wake himself up and then cursed some more when he saw the time on the cuckoo clock hanging on one of the living room walls. Nine fifty a.m. *Shit.* He had work to do today. He never overslept.

Ding-dong. Ding-dong.

Christian swung open the front door and found Abby on the other side. At the same time, Jonah appeared from the other direction of the house—with only a towel wrapped low around his waist. *Holy hell.* Christian's throat immediately went dry. Jonah's skin glistened with moisture, and his dark hair lay plastered against his head. The man had the widest shoulders Christian had ever seen, and a giant tattoo of what looked like a wing covered his entire left shoulder, down the upper part of his arm, and surely his back too. The tattoo was large but simple, done in black lines with only a hint of shading at the peak of each feather, but it immediately drew Christian's eye. Jonah's stomach rippled with cuts and grooves, and part of another tattoo peeked out from under the towel. Whatever the design, it looked like it sat center on his lower belly.

Holy hell. Again.

"Oh"—Jonah stopped midstep—"you're awake. I was in the shower." He shrugged his massive shoulders. "Obviously. I heard the doorbell and came to answer it."

Christian shook his head and tore his focus off Jonah's stomach. *Damn.* "I've got it."

A little light twinkled silver in Jonah's eyes. "I see that."

Heat flared under Christian's skin. "Right."

"And if you could let me inside," Abby said, drawing Christian's attention back to her, "that would be great. I'm here with breakfast"—she held up a big paper bag—"and a moving van." She stepped aside and waved her arm in the direction of the driveway. "I'm ready to get started whenever you are."

Christian rubbed his neck. "Started with what?"

Abby looked from Christian to Jonah and back to Christian. She stared at Christian and put her head on a tilt. "Getting rid of Mari's stuff, of course."

The heat under Christian's skin grew into a fire, and his hunched shoulders disappeared in a flash. "Who in the hell told you we were doing that?"

Jonah cleared his throat, and Christian whipped around to face the man.

With eyes piercing, and his arms crossed against his chest, Jonah said, "I did."

Chapter Three

I did.

Fury spread the fire in Christian's belly to an inferno. He stormed over to Jonah and lifted up on tiptoe in order to get right in his face. "Who in the hell do you think you are, coming in here the day before Mari's funeral, pushing your way into her house"—Jonah reared back at that, but Christian didn't slow down one bit—"and then sticking around without even asking if it's okay, thinking you have the right to decide what happens to her house and her stuff?" Christian got in so close, he bumped his chest into Jonah's, searing bare skin to bare skin, but even that couldn't stop him. "*I* lived here until I graduated from high school. *I* never lost touch with Mari—"

Jonah suddenly pushed back, intimidating with his much bigger body. "*Neither. Did. I.*" He bit off each word and shoved them down Christian's throat. "Never once. Not in all the years since the cops took me away from this house."

"What?" The tension in Christian went slack, and he stumbled. Jonah grabbed him and settled him against the back of the couch. His head swirling, Christian looked around the living room, searching for something that must have always been there, but that he had somehow overlooked. Mari had pride in her foster children. Of the ones who remained in touch, she had mementos all over the home to show her joy. Christian studied the many photos again, but nothing that even slightly resembled Jonah lived on her living room walls.

Coming back to Jonah, Christian looked up and found Jonah's gaze—pale but somehow not angry, even after Christian's cutting judgment. Christian locked his hands in a tight hold behind his neck. *Once again, I made myself look like an idiot in front of this man. Damn it.*

"I-I just don't understand," Christian began. "There's nothing of you here, and she never said anything"—his attention flicked briefly to Abby, who shook her head—"to any of us, apparently."

His jaw ticking, Jonah let his focus move around the walls full of pictures. "Probably because I never gave her anything. When I got out of JD and headed south, I never actually saw her in person again. Maybe I didn't want her to have anything. I don't know." Jonah rubbed his jaw, scratching through a day's worth of stubble. With his attention somewhere behind Christian's right shoulder, he said, "Probably just never occurred to me to give her a picture. Can't really think of any I have of myself, actually. I don't really think of stuff like that."

God, the guy just emanates solitude. Disturbed, Christian crossed his legs so that he didn't go to Jonah and touch his face. He rubbed at the hairs tickling the back of his neck instead. "So Mari went and saw you while you were in jail?"

Still not making eye contact, Jonah nodded, and he spoke through tight lips. "Marisol came to visit me every month while I was in JD." His shoulder and chest muscles tightened, and he abruptly crossed his arms. "I didn't give her a lot of reasons to be hopeful about my cause, but she never tossed me away. When I got out and moved to Miami, I stayed in touch with her as best I could. It may not have been what you did, or even what Abby did, and truthfully, I don't know, maybe it wasn't enough, but I still felt compelled to come here and honor her life. She requested that I do. I won't leave until I see her final wish carried out."

Christian shot back upright. "Hey! I don't intend to shirk Mari's wishes. I will get this house fixed up and sold."

"I'm not saying you won't, damn it!" Jonah jammed his fingers through his wet hair and took a decided step away from Christian. He looked Christian in the eyes, but there wasn't a bit of cold in the icy color, just pure, *intoxicating* life. Christian inhaled sharply, creating an audible gasp.

Jonah zeroed in on Christian's reaction right away. His shoulders rolled forward in a slump, and he exhaled a shaky breath. "I apologize." He took yet another step back. "I didn't mean to yell at you. I get louder than I think I am sometimes."

A tight band squeezed around Christian's middle. Memories of a big, angry teenager who never belittled or shoved around his much-smaller roommate washed over Christian, overriding everything else. He pushed away from the couch and put himself within hitting range of Jonah. "You didn't scare me. I'm not afraid to incite your anger just because of your past."

Jonah leaned back, almost as if he were suddenly afraid Christian would touch him. "Look"—Jonah paused and strung together a handful of curse words—"I was only trying to help. I could see how hard yesterday was for you. I brought food home, but you had already crashed, before nine o'clock. I know how tight you were with Mari, and I would guess that would make it extra hard to part with her stuff. I thought if I could get some of the first steps started, then it might be easier for you. I don't intend to empty her house and drive everything to the dump. I thought we could give the furniture to Goodwill, and the clothes to the church. I found Abby and Rodrigo's numbers in Marisol's phone book last night and called them. Abby says she can go through the jewelry and see what she might be able to sell in her shop."

"To give the money to one of her favorite charities, of course," Abby said, from where she still stood on the porch. Abby owned a vintage clothing shop, where she also sold her own jewelry creations. "Not to keep for myself."

"Right." Jonah nodded. "And I called Rodrigo because he actually showed up at the funeral yesterday to lend you support, which made me think he cared and would be open to helping. I didn't realize he was a contractor and would be able to not only help us with the floors, the walls, maybe even new siding, but that he can get some of the materials we'll need at cost." Jonah suddenly looked stricken, and he quickly added, "Rodrigo volunteered to do it. I didn't threaten or intimidate him in any way."

Christian smiled wryly. "Don't worry. I didn't think you did. Rodrigo wouldn't be intimidated by anyone, anyway. He's not necessarily a nice man all the time, but he is always a *good* man."

Right in front of Christian, Jonah's skin went flush, and he dropped his attention to the floor. "Oh," he said, his voice hushed.

Christian's chest constricted. Could Jonah care that Christian thought so well of another man? "Rodrigo is my boss," Christian explained. "That's why I can say with authority that he's a good person."

Jonah's focus shot right back up to Christian. "Oh," he said again. The edge of his lip even turned up with a small smile.

Christian's heart started to race, and he couldn't look away. "Yeah."

"He didn't tell me that when I talked to him. He just agreed to help."

"Well, whatever he said or didn't say"—Abby's voice tore through the moment, breaking Christian's gaze off Jonah. She stood sideways and stared in the direction of the driveway—"he's here." She glanced at her watch. "Right on time."

A few seconds later, Rodrigo filled the doorway next to Abby, wearing jeans, a white T-shirt, and a dark pair of sunglasses. Slipping the sunglasses off and hooking them over the crew neck of his shirt, Rodrigo assessed Abby first, whereupon she crossed her bare arms. Christian swore that the woman, who was no petite thing next to Rodrigo's six-plus-feet of height, would have stretched her shorts and yanked the fabric halfway down her uncovered legs, if she could.

That done, Rodrigo glanced through the screen door to Christian, and Jonah and gave an equally probing, raised-eyebrow look. "Do I need to take something off before we get to work? Could be interesting, but I tend to like to have certain key body parts fully protected when I know I'm gonna be handling power tools. But hey"—he flashed a smile that made him look truly wicked—"that's just me."

Jonah turned beet red and clutched the towel around his waist. "Shit." Clearly, it just hit him that he stood in front of three people in only that one scrap of terry cloth. "Let me go shave and get dressed, and we'll get started." He turned a level stare on Christian. "As long as it's okay with you?"

God, Christian really didn't want to pack up this house. To honor Mari's wishes, he went ahead and nodded anyway. "Yeah, it's good." At least he didn't have to make these first difficult steps himself. "Thank you for doing it."

Jonah dipped his head. "Good."

As Jonah turned and moved to the back of the house, Christian couldn't help his gaze straying to the fine shape of the man's tight ass, covered only by one white towel.

Rodrigo cleared his throat very loudly from the porch. With his face heating, Christian unlatched the lock on the screen door and let Abby and Rodrigo inside.

* * *

Jonah eyed Christian where he stood, staring at the photos mapping the walls of Marisol's living room. Christian looked like the pictures had put him in a trance, and Jonah suffered an attack of uncertainty, something he rarely experienced in his life—at least until showing up back in Coleman three days ago.

Sighing, Jonah locked his hands behind his back. He had to, or he feared he might slip in behind Christian and pull the man against his chest. And Jonah just *did not* experience urges like that in his normal life.

"We don't have to do this tonight, you know." Jonah broke the silence that hung heavy in the air. "If you're not ready, we can put the walls off and do the floors first."

Before Abby and Rodrigo left for the evening, Christian had told them he would take down all the pictures so they could get started tearing the paneling down first thing tomorrow. Today, in addition to a hundred little cleaning issues, they had boxed up Marisol's clothing and taken it down to the church. Abby went through the jewelry and took it to her store, confident in her ability to sell it for a nice piece of change. They also made use of the moving van and removed all the furniture from the house, except for the table and chairs in the kitchen, as well as the beds and low bookshelf from the room Jonah and Christian had so briefly shared as kids. Tonight, they would share that small space again.

Right now, though, Jonah didn't think bunking together had crossed Christian's mind once.

Christian stood silently with his arms locked at his sides, still staring at the wall as if Jonah had never spoken. "Okay," Jonah said abruptly, making a decision for the pair of them, "you don't need to do this tonight. I'm used to being all sweaty and gross." He felt like grime an inch thick covered his T-shirt and jeans. "So why don't you hit the shower first? I'll go get us food while you're doing that."

"No." Christian's hand snapped out and locked around Jonah's wrist, without moving his head or any other part of his body. "We can do this right now. I'm fine."

Jonah's skin burned where Christian had him manacled. It snaked lines of pure sexual awareness throughout his body and had his voice sounding grittier than usual. "You sure?"

"Yeah. I'm just thinking about all the people in these pictures, and how I never even met most of them, yet I feel like I know them because of the stories Mari used to tell me. It's strange to have this gut sense of knowing...what"—he waved his other hand along the wall—"more than fifty people whom I've never actually put eyes on in my life. Granted, I know most of them had slipped to just sending a birthday or Christmas card every year, but they are my family in a weird way because they never left Mari's heart." Christian's voice softened, and his fingers twined down into Jonah's, locking in a tight handhold. Jonah almost forgot how to breathe. Nobody had ever held his hand before. "When this house sells, it's going to be very strange not to come here twice a week for dinner and feel the personalities that seem to live in the walls that make you feel like you belong." He turned his head and found Jonah's gaze. Christian's eyes were dry, and he had a wistful kind of smile on his face. "I just wanted to take a few minutes to honor that and acknowledge that it is a very big deal. I wasn't objecting to the task."

Never before had Jonah fought tears because of another person. For the life of him, he didn't want Christian to ever let go of his hand either. "You're honorable." Jonah somehow found words, although he didn't know how he got them past the tightness in his throat. "I think that's why Marisol felt such a bond to you. She saw a kindred spirit, another special soul."

"What? No—"

A knock at the door put a halt to Christian's words.

Jonah yanked his hand out of Christian's, and they both spun to the open door. They had turned off the air-conditioning because of the all-day in-and-out traffic of their task, and right now, only the screen door protected them from the outside, the only thing between them and the blond guy from the church.

David.

Jonah's temperature rose ten degrees just seeing the man again.

David lifted his hand in an abbreviated wave. "Chris. Hi." His attention slid briefly to Jonah. "Hello again." He said only that and went right back to looking at Christian.

Jonah barely contained a snarl and a growl.

Christian took a step forward but abruptly stopped. "What are you doing here?"

Shoving his hands into the pockets of his khaki shorts, David looked at Jonah again. When he came back to Christian, he made a beckoning gesture with his shoulder. "Can we talk outside for a minute?" He smiled, but it looked forced. "I won't take much of your time. I promise."

Christian clenched and unclenched his fists, and then rubbed his palms on his jeans. "We've said everything that needs saying, David. I've already told you that."

"I'd like to apologize to you for my behavior yesterday," David said, his focus zeroing right in on Christian. "If you'll give me a chance."

Jonah watched a deep breath fill Christian before he slowly exhaled. "You have two minutes," he answered as he walked to the door. "That's it."

David dipped his head. "Thank you. That's all I need."

Christian stepped onto the porch, and with a slew of foul language, Jonah slipped to the wall beside the door and plastered his back to it. *Idiot, you're not a thirteen-year-old girl. You have no right to invade Christian's privacy like this.* Even as Jonah thought it, and didn't know what in the hell he was doing—*I don't give a shit about other people's personal business!*—he couldn't tear his spine off the paneled wall and move out of listening distance.

Jonah recognized David's voice first. "I'm sorry I cornered you at Marisol's funeral. I don't know what I was thinking. It wasn't right, and it never should have happened."

"Fine," Christian said, his tone terse. "Apology accepted. You can go home now."

"While I shouldn't have done it there"—David's words spilled out in a rush—"the reason I did it holds true. I know you're hurting over this loss. I want you to come to me when you need someone to talk to. I want to be there for you."

"I don't need your shoulder. I am fine." Christian sounded tired, and Jonah locked his legs in place so that he didn't charge through the door and shove David right off Marisol's porch. "You need to be there for your wife, not me."

"But she—"

"I don't care. 'But she'…nothing," Christian said.

Jonah couldn't actually see Christian, but he bet the man had his hands clasped behind his neck. Jonah had already noticed Christian tended to do that when upset.

"Listen to me, David," Christian went on. "I shouldn't have to tell you this, but here I am doing it. You are a married man. You have committed yourself to a woman. You made that choice, and now it is up to you to honor it."

"I've never wanted anyone but you, and I damn well know you want me just as much. We are magic together. Do you need me to remind you some of the things you said to me while I had your ass open and begging for—"

"I'm not denying any of what we had," Christian interrupted. Jonah could hear the exhaustion in the man's voice. "I never did deny it. You were the one who did, and by doing so made your choice loud and clear with your actions, all of which screamed much louder than your words. I stayed with you too long as it was, once I realized you were dating that woman. Not anymore. I aided in your being a cheater, but I will not help you become an adulterer. If you can't live without dick, get it somewhere else. You can't have mine anymore. If I have to tell you that one more time, if you come to this house, my apartment, or one of my job sites again, I will file a harassment report and you won't have to worry about hiding your preferences from your wife. She'll find out about it from the cops when they arrest you. Don't do that to her. She's a nice woman. Either get divorced or commit to the marriage. But no matter what you do, I won't be a part of your life anymore. Get that through your head, once and for all." Christian yanked open the screen door. "Go home, David. Good-bye."

Christian shut the door and locked it, but his fingers shook. He jerked as his gaze collided with Jonah's, where Jonah still stood, not three feet away from the door.

Stiffening, Christian made a threatening lean in toward Jonah. "You got something you want to say?"

One thing swirled in Jonah's mind, and it built up a crazy fluttering in his blood. Unable to ignore it, he said, "I didn't hear you say you weren't in love with him anymore." Christ, Jonah's chest hurt, and he fucking didn't like it, but he had to ask. "Do you still love David?"

Chapter Four

As soon as the question, "Do you still love David?" left Jonah's mouth, he wanted to grab it back and shove it down inside him, away from the ears of others. Away from Christian. Christian opened his mouth, but Jonah overrode him with, "Never mind. David is your business. You've already told me once to respect that, and I will. I apologize."

Twin lines of red bloomed under Christian's deep tan skin, burnishing his cheeks. "So then you did hear everything."

Jonah clenched his jaw but forced honesty past his lips. "That's the reason I moved to the wall." Christian's eyes widened with Jonah's confession. Hating the personal exposure, so unfamiliar, Jonah still couldn't look away or stop. "I don't like the man; I won't lie about that. Do you know how many guys—I'm talking teenagers here—were locked up because they got obsessed about someone and couldn't take no for an answer? David may seem harmless enough on the outside, but I've seen smaller, less-aggressive-looking men than him in jail for horrific acts. Be careful with him. If he really does bother you again, don't let that threat you made be an empty one. File a report and request a restraining order, and don't let him violate it."

Christian chewed on a hangnail, nodding. "I know. I don't think it will come to that, though. He is living a lie, but he won't risk his marriage to change it. He won't risk being outed to his family, his wife, his wife's family, and all of his friends. He just won't." Abruptly, Christian turned to the wall and removed the first frame. He opened the back to take the photo out and then wrapped the frame for donation. Jonah moved to do the same, assuming their conversation had ended.

The rustle of newspaper filled the quiet, and for long minutes, they worked in companionable silence. Then Christian said softly, "Do you want me to answer your question?"

No. Jonah squeezed his eyes shut for a second. "Yes."

A weary-sounding sigh reached Jonah's ears. "The truth is," Christian shared, "I'm not sure if I ever was in love with him." Jonah caught Christian glance his way, and he held the younger man's stare for a long, drawn-out moment. Christian darted his focus back to the wall, cleared his throat, and took down another picture. "We played baseball together in high school, and I developed a crush on him; I know that much. We became friends, and I trusted him. Maybe I sensed he was gay, and maybe part of the attraction was that I knew there was at least the *possibility* he could like me back. When I was cut from the minors after injuring my knee, I came back home, and David and I immediately picked up our friendship. Eventually, it turned sexual. David wanted to keep it a secret, which I understood. But when I realized he was openly dating a woman and hinting to others that it was serious, I faced that he wouldn't ever come out of the closet for me. I broke it off." Christian's voice grew stronger with every sentence he spoke, and to Jonah's eyes it looked like he stood taller too. "That was over a year ago. Six months later, David got married to that woman; her name is Carrie. Three months ago, he came to me wanting to pick things up again. I refused, and that really threw him. He's having a hard time accepting no."

As much as Jonah already hated David, he had to assume the guy wasn't all bad if Christian let their relationship go as far as he had. He must have *something* in him worth liking. Maybe still did. Jonah's gut clenched, instantly rejecting the notion. *Jealousy.* It heated his belly. He'd never experienced the burn of it before, and he fucking didn't like it. Almost as if in punishment, he asked, "What if David came to you, said he would leave his wife, and agreed to be open with you? Would you go back to him then?"

"No," Christian answered, without hesitation. He looked to Jonah, a sudden smile on his face. "Huh." He tilted his head. "I guess that's my answer. If I were still in love with him, or ever was, I probably would go back to him. But I won't, no matter the circumstances. It is over, for good."

Cool relief blanketed the heat inside Jonah. The sensation was another first for him: his comfort and mood sitting at the mercy of another person's choices. "Let's hope for your sake David got the message tonight." *The man better damn well listen to Christian this time.* Jonah might not be able to restrain himself if David kept pushing. He remembered too many horror stories from other guys in JD, and he shook off a chill that sliced down his spine.

"I hope he did too." Christian found Jonah's gaze and held it. "How about you?" he asked, a soft catch in his voice. "Do you have anyone special down in Miami? Have you ever been in love?"

"Uhh…" The blood drained from Jonah's face; he could feel the sudden cold. He had never cared before, but right now, his insides cramped, making him feel sick with the thought that Christian would ever know how detached Jonah felt from everyone else in the world. "We should get back to work." His voice came across even harder than usual, but he couldn't control the roughness. "We have a lot of pictures to remove and frames to wrap before the night is over."

Christian blinked and turned away, fumbling a picture as he pulled it off the wall. "Sorry." Snatching the frame off the pile of newspapers where it fell, he flipped it over and worked the latches, struggling to get them open.

Damn it. Don't tell him. Just shut up. "No." Jonah bit off the one word. *Fuck.* Christian had given him a perfectly good out. "There isn't anyone at home. I've never been in love." He put his full concentration on removing a photo of Marisol and Abby from a light wood frame. "Not sure I know what it is."

"Oh," Christian said. Out of the corner of his eye, Jonah caught Christian rubbing his neck. "Okay."

Jonah bit down the desire to try to explain himself, which would only dig him an even deeper hole. "Okay."

"Okay."

They went back to work, the silence thick at first, but eventually the tension lessened and Jonah started to breathe a little easier.

A good half hour later, Christian murmured, "Thank you for telling me that."

Jonah's legs weakened at Christian words. *Maybe he doesn't think I'm a freak after all.* Right on top of that, pure need, unlike anything Jonah had ever experienced, rushed through his blood fast enough to dizzy him. Everything in him wanted to grab Christian, crowd him into the wall, and fuse their mouths and bodies into one.

Clutching the frame in his hands hard enough to snap it in two, Jonah said only, "No problem."

* * *

"Damn, I'm tired." Christian dropped to the floor and laid himself out flat, uncaring of the mess littering most of the living room. Sweat covered every inch of his skin. He knew he smelled to high heaven, but right now, he could not move another muscle. Christian was used to backbreaking work, but doing these renovations for Mari's home felt more draining than any job he'd ever done for Rodrigo, or even than his longest seventeen-inning marathon game in the minors. He needed to push himself up and drag his ass to the shower; instead, he rolled over on his side as Jonah reentered the room.

"Here you go." Jonah, just as dirty as Christian, handed over an ice-cold bottle of water. He eased down on the floor as well, groaning as he stretched out. He put his own bottle of water on the floor, stacked his hands behind his head, and shifted his attention Christian's way. "You want to use the shower first, or should I?"

Christian yawned, even though it was only eight o'clock. "Excuse me." He covered his mouth after the fact. All of his muscles, but particularly his lower back, loudly protested his getting up. "You go ahead and use it. I can wait."

"Okay." Jonah stretched his arms and legs, making more noises as his muscles popped and strained. Jonah's matter-of-fact movements showed off the tone of his fit body in a way that made Christian salivate. The shift pulled at the edge of Jonah's T-shirt, exposing a sliver of his belly, all flat, hard, and perfect. The man started to lift up, hung stiff for a moment, and then lay right back down. Jonah darted a glance at Christian, and Christian noticed a sting of red on Jonah's cheeks along with a half smile. Both grabbed tight at Christian's chest. Jonah murmured, "Maybe I'll get up in a minute."

Christian chuckled. "Or maybe you won't." They were both acting like a couple of old men with rickety bodies. Thank God Christian had decided to live in Mari's home for the duration of this renovation and had brought toiletries and plenty of clothes over from his apartment. Two days into the job and he already couldn't imagine having to climb into his truck every night to crash at his apartment. He was starting to think Jonah wouldn't fare any safer driving back to a motel.

"You're right. I might not get up after all." Jonah laughed back, a rusty-sounding noise that made Christian think the man didn't make the sound often. "Damn." Jonah reached to

his right and pulled a pile of folded tarps to his side. "Here"—
he handed half the stack to Christian—"put that under your
neck. You look like your head is about to drop off your
shoulders." Jonah used the other half for himself. "It's not
like I don't work fourteen-hours days on a regular basis back
home, but fuck, the job we started today killed my back and
arms. I may not stand straight for a week." They had spent
the day removing paneling and scraping glue off the walls.

"You'll move soon enough, whether you want to or not."
Christian kneaded his neck and shoulder, easing the tension
there. "Rodrigo never gets tired or sore. Trust me, he'll be
here bright and early tomorrow to get us right back on
schedule."

"Do you like working for him?" Jonah asked. Through
conversation during their second full day of renovating the
house, talk had naturally turned to Rodrigo's contractor
work. "What about the baseball?" Jonah turned to his side
and faced Christian. "I removed a good number of pictures of
you in various minor league uniforms last night."

"One of them was from the majors," Christian shared,
grinning at the memory. "I played with the Cardinals for six
weeks when I was twenty-two."

"No shit." Jonah slipped his hands under his cheek,
mirroring Christian. Animation shone in Jonah's pale eyes,
an interest that warmed Christian's blood—and twitched his
cock. *God, he's so rough and beautiful.*

"I didn't realize you'd gone pro." Jonah's voice snapped
Christian out of his fantasizing. "What happened?"

A soft smile edged Christian's lips. "In '02, the Cards
were in the postseason hunt when the roster number gets

raised near the end of the regular season. I was in their organization, and they brought me up." Christian drifted back to the highlight of his baseball career, to stepping out on that pristine field for the first time, the awe and shiver that sat just under the surface of his skin through the entire first week of playing in the show. "When we made it into the postseason, the team kept me on the roster. It shocked the hell out of me. We were knocked out in the Championship Series by the Giants, though, unfortunately. I batted a couple of key runs in with a few doubles, and I had one home run, so I did okay. Anyway, I went back to the minors the next season and injured my knee. I never could recover it enough to get back up to base-running speed. I wasn't a good enough hitter for a team in the American League to hire me on as a designated hitter. The injury essentially ended my career, and I came home."

"Wow." Reverence laced Jonah's voice, and Christian felt it like a long caress down his back. "Even that short amount of time is a pretty big deal. Millions of kids dream about playing in the pros, in any sport, and you were actually there."

Christian shrugged, needing to brush off the sensation of Jonah's phantom touch. It wasn't even real, yet it reached deeper inside Christian than anything David had ever done to him. Shaking his head, Christian forced himself to focus. "It was fun feeling like a big deal for a month and a half while I was there. I like my life now, though, just as much. I like working with Rodrigo."

Jonah stiffened. "No. Damn. I didn't mean to imply that you don't or that it's less important." Rolling onto his back,

Jonah dug his fingers into his mess of dark hair. "Fuck, I fix bikes and custom cars for a living. Why would I judge that you fix houses? I wasn't saying you should be prouder of one thing than the other."

"And I didn't mean anything by clarifying that I like working for Rodrigo. I was just sharing information." Christian looked the rigid man up and down, frustration lacing his own body. "Why do you get so defensive and jump to an assumption that I'm judging you all the time? We're just talking."

Jonah stayed looking up at the ceiling. Eventually, he exhaled, long and slow. "I'm not very good at it."

"What?"

"Talking." Jonah's hands fell to his sides. He grabbed at the tarp covering the flooring and twisted it in his fingers. "When you're in JD, you have to guard yourself against other guys working an angle. For me, when I wasn't learning a trade or taking courses, I listened and watched more than I talked. Now, when I'm at work, I talk about bikes and engines and cars, whatever is needed to get a job done. When I go home at night, I eat, maybe workout or watch some TV, and go to sleep. When I have sex, I have sex; I don't talk before or after I do it. I don't know how to talk just to get to know someone." Jonah's jaw ticked at the back, and his voice dropped low. "Or how to let them get to know me."

Every line of Jonah's body lay strung tight, and Christian wanted nothing so much as to ease this man's obvious discomfort. Christian dealt with uncertainty and fear every time he shared his homosexuality with a new person, but he somehow didn't think his worst day even remotely compared to how Jonah viewed himself every day. Everything about the sudden insight broke Christian's heart.

His fingers trembling, Christian reached out and touched Jonah's forearm. Jonah's breath caught. He jerked and latched his gaze onto Christian's. The heat searing Jonah's skin shot electricity through Christian's fingers and all through his body, but Christian forced himself not to pull away from the sizzle. "You could start by not assuming that your size or your time in JD is the first and only thing on people's minds when they talk to you. It isn't, you know."

Jonah's pupils flared, but he didn't break the eye contact. "Fair enough. And maybe you can ease up on the defensiveness with fixing Marisol's home and just believe I want to help you, and that I'm not trying to take over or tell you what's best to do."

Christian dipped his head as heat suffused his skin. "Fair enough," he mimicked. His palm still buzzing with the touch of Jonah's skin, Christian slid his hand down Jonah's arm and clasped his hand. "Do we have a deal?"

It seemed like Jonah lay there frozen for eons, so long Christian's palm started to sweat within Jonah's grasp. Suddenly embarrassed that maybe he had pushed this renewed friendship too fast, Christian tried to disentangle his hand from Jonah's.

Right then, Jonah closed down around Christian's fingers. With gruffness that Christian was starting to think was Jonah's normal, Jonah finally said, "We have a deal."

This time, Christian let out the shaky breath. "All right. Good."

"Good."

Jonah didn't let go of Christian's hand. He stayed with Christian's gaze too. Slowly, everything around them blurred, and for Christian, only Jonah's face and hand remained. For the life of him, Christian could not tear himself away from Jonah's smoky eyes, even when he swore Jonah shifted their handshake and entwined their fingers in a different kind of hold.

A more intimate hold.

Christian's breathing shifted to something shallower, but his heart didn't race crazily or out of control. The clamminess left his palms too. Everything inside Christian slowed, and the very air around them embraced him in a sense of safety and comfort that defied even what Mari had given him as a kid.

Looking into Jonah's eyes, inch by inch, even the man's face became a blur, and eventually, holding hands, exhaustion caught up to him, and Christian drifted to sleep.

* * *

Christian sat, Indian-style, in the nook of space between his bed and a low bookshelf. He held an open comic in his lap and tried to focus on the superhero story. Even though the hero was full of muscles and kind of sexy, Christian didn't think the man was nearly as cute as his roommate. Nobody looked as good as Jonah.

The bedroom door opened barely a dozen inches, and the object of Christian's thoughts slipped inside. Jonah closed the door with careful hands—big, wonderful hands, Christian thought—and leaned against the wood, softly banging his head. His chest heaved with a rapid rise and fall, and he muttered, "Stupid, stupid, stupid," with each tap of his head against the door.

"You're in trouble again, aren't you?"

Jonah jumped and whirled, scanning the small room until he found Christian in the shadows. "Jesus, Christian"— Jonah advanced on him—"you scared the shit out of me." The older boy dropped to his knees in front of Christian, and Christian spotted the wildness in Jonah's gaze right away, something far beyond his normal belligerence. "You shouldn't be reading in the dark, kid; you're gonna hurt your eyes." He slipped the *X-Men* comic out of Christian's hand and dog-eared the page before sliding it on the bookshelf. "Listen"—sweat poured down Jonah's temples, over his neck, and into his shirt—"I need a few minutes by myself." He leaned over and reached under his bed, pulling out his backpack before standing up and heading to the dresser. "Can you give me the room?"

Christian's focus darted all up and down Jonah, taking in the signs of stress that went well beyond the ticks and traits he had obsessively observed in Jonah over the last few months.

Scrambling to his feet, Christian rushed to Jonah and grabbed his arm. "You're in trouble, aren't you?" he asked again, his voice trembling this time. He jutted his chin as he looked up at Jonah. "The cops are gonna come and take you to jail, aren't they?"

Jonah paused, the gray in his eyes turning to charcoal. "Sometimes you're too smart for your own good." He grabbed a tuft of Christian's hair and tilted his head back, forcing eye contact he rarely gave to anyone. "You don't want to know what kind of stupid-ass, shit mess I'm in. You have to get out of here and let me do what I need to do. I don't want you getting into trouble with the boss lady."

No, I don't want you to go! Panic and loss raced through Christian, trying to force out tears. Just as quickly, he stuffed them down and grabbed Jonah's arm, yanking the older boy's hand out of his hair. "I can help you." He dragged Jonah to the window with all his might. "Here, help me move the bookshelf." Christian let go and wedged into his nook, grasping one end of the heavy piece of furniture on his own and started to push. "You can climb out the window. There's a hole in the fence at the back that goes through to a house on Leroy Street. From there you can start running through that field one more block over, until you reach the interstate. You can hitch a ride or walk down in the ditches or behind the trees until you hit another town, and you can take a bus out of Florida." Christian suddenly came to a stop. "Wait, I have some money I earned mowing lawns. I can give it to you." He dropped to the floor and slid halfway under the bed.

"Wait, wait." Jonah grabbed Christian's leg and dragged him back out. Pulling him upright, Jonah stood Christian in front of him. "No, you can't do this. I won't let you do this."

"But I have to."

Jonah grabbed Christian's shoulders and forced him to stop. "You don't." His voice, always full of impatience, rang with authority. "You're a good kid, and I'm not going to let you get into trouble for helping me."

"I have money." Christian struggled to get out of Jonah's hold. "I can help you."

With a sharp shake, Jonah brought Christian's fight to a stop. "I don't want you to help me," he whispered furiously. "I just want you to forget you ever knew me."

"No." Christian shook his head, fighting tears that would make him look like a baby and remind Jonah that he was still only fourteen. He reached up and covered Jonah's hands, not letting him break contact. Jonah's skin was rough and warm. The touch tingled through Christian's palm, reminding him just how special Jonah was to him. "I can't forget you."

Jonah looked away and threw out a colorful mix of curses before shaking his head and coming back to Christian. "You can." His voice sounded extra thick, his eyes looked a little too bright, and both things twisted at Christian's confused heart. "And you will." Jonah squeezed Christian's neck and, with his superior strength, pulled away. "I've gotta go."

"Wait!" Christian grabbed Jonah's T-shirt, his mind and heart racing out of control. Life buzzed under his skin, and he couldn't unlock his hands and let Jonah leave. "Just wait."

Jonah stayed in place but sighed and shifted his weight from one foot to the other. "Make it fast, Christian." He covered Christian's hands with his bigger ones, working to pry his fingers under Christian's death grip to free his shirt. "I have to go."

I'll never get another chance. Keeping his eyes open wide, Christian yanked Jonah down and smashed his lips against the older boy's in a hard, crushing first kiss. Christian held on tight, fused his mouth to Jonah's, and his heart soared.

* * *

Suddenly, everything swirled within Christian, and he was no longer that fourteen-year-old boy with a crush, nor was Jonah the angry teen trying to flee the law. Christian's body, mind, and heart fast-forwarded to the present day, and he writhed against the length of a fully grown Jonah—who kissed Christian back with hot, searing kisses. They fell onto Christian's bed together as tongues tangled and moans filled the air, chasing away any lingering memories from fifteen years ago. The full-on adult kiss was everything Christian ever wanted from Jonah. As he sank into it, opening up for more, his cock raged hard in his jeans, begging for relief.

Christian groaned with need he could not deny. He tore at the snap and zipper on his jeans, laying the flaps open so that only his underwear covered his cock. He broke the kiss and stared through lust-filled eyes at the blur of Jonah in front of him. "Touch me." His penis pushed hard against the fabric of his briefs. "Help me come."

"Oh, fuck." Jonah lunged and plastered his lips to Christian's in an aggressive, taking kiss. He shoved his hand down into Christian's underwear at the same time, covering Christian's prick and taking it in his hand with a hard pull. Christian gasped with shock and joy, and Jonah used that as an opening to deepen the kiss with invasive, *wonderful* thrusts from his tongue. Jonah rubbed up and down the length of Christian's cock with full drags, the coarseness of his hand on Christian's dick painfully exquisite. Christian swore he could feel the dozens of little nicks littering Jonah's fingertips, imperfections that Christian had noticed the first day they met and that still existed today. Christian pumped his hips for more of Jonah's rough touch; Jonah complied and tugged harder, getting all the slickness he needed for the handjob from Christian himself.

Christian grew harder than he had ever been before, and his balls ached, heavy with cum. "Oh, God, more," he mumbled breathlessly against Jonah's lips, licking them, as he'd so often dreamed of doing. "More, Jonah, more."

Jonah moaned something unintelligible against Christian's mouth and then buried his hand between Christian's thighs, grabbing his nuts and rolling them in his hand. He alternated the hold on Christian's sac with rubbing the tips of his blunt fingers across the sensitive skin of Christian's inner thighs. Christian shivered and bucked, crying out when Jonah went right back to his cock and yanked it from root to tip, spiraling Christian into full-on, shaking release. "Ahh, yeah, yeah, coming..." Christian pumped his hips with every spurt of seed, sliding his cock within the snug hold of Jonah's hand with each wave of orgasm that rocked through him. Every ounce of blood coursed with life and every nerve ending sat right on the edge, through to the final wave, until finally his heart rate started to decelerate and his muscles went lax.

Eventually, other sensations in Christian's body pushed front and center, sending frissons of a different kind of awareness down his spine. Numbness from sleeping on a hard floor tingled up the right side of his body, and his neck tensed with a tight ache, reminding him he didn't sleep in a bed with a mattress and a pillow. *Oh, right.* He was on the living room floor where he had fallen asleep without making it to bed.

Holding Jonah's hand.

Christian's eyes popped open as the memory rushed through him, sobering him to full alertness. Jonah's gray gaze waited for him in the shadows, fully open and aware, some two feet away.

That wasn't nearly the worst of it.

Christian had Jonah's hand in a lock hold, buried inside his jeans, against his cock.

And yes, Christian really had come.

Chapter Five

Oh God. Oh God. Oh God.

Christian had Jonah's fingers clutched under his, *forcing* them against his cock. Moreover, Christian had just come, right in Jonah's hand.

Oh God. Oh God. Oh God.

Suddenly, Christian shoved Jonah's hand out of his jeans, as if they were both on fire. The sheen of ejaculate coated Jonah's fingers, undeniable evidence of what Christian had done.

Oh God. Oh God. Oh God.

Christian wiped his hand on his shirt and struggled to get his zipper done up at least, mortified to his core. "I'm sorry. I don't know what I was thinking." His heart racing, Christian looked all around the living room, anywhere but at Jonah or the dark stain on the front of his own jeans. He wasn't sure he would ever be able to look Jonah in the eyes again. "It must have just been normal morning bodily actions. I had your hand when I fell asleep so I must have just shoved it down—"

"You said my name."

Christian jerked back, Jonah's statement turning his focus up to the man's hard face once again after all. Completely unreadable, Jonah stared at Christian, his expression a virtual blank slate. Christian shook his head, trying to keep his attention off that damn shine on Jonah's fingers, his shame on full display.

"Wh-wh—" Christian cleared his throat and tried again. "What?"

Shifting forward, Jonah closed half the distance between them, instantly heating the already-humid air around them, making it downright difficult to breathe. His focus dropped to Christian's crotch, staying there long enough to make Christian sweat, as well as his cock shift visibly behind his jeans, hardening again already. Jonah's chest rose and fell in a deep wave. When he finally brought his gaze back up to Christian's, his skin was ruddy, and his irises were thin circles of mercury around fathomless, dark pupils. "After you shoved my hand against your dick," Jonah shared, "you said my name."

Unable to look away, Christian's throat scratched like a desert and his heart pounded erratically. *He is so close right now.* One shift forward and Christian could claim Jonah's mouth, making that part of his dream real too. Damn it, he wanted to taste Jonah in the worst possible way. Need overcame sense, and Christian leaned forward into Jonah's heat—

The doorbell chimed. Christian and Jonah jerked, banging heads.

"Perfect." Christian fell backward as stinging tingles rippled over his scalp and slid down his neck, creating misshapen spots in front of his eyes. He didn't know whether to thank Rodrigo—because without looking at his watch, Christian knew it must be eight o'clock on the dot—or put a curse on the punctual man. Digging the heels of his hands into his eyes, he muttered, "My day is starting out absolutely perfect."

Jonah rolled smoothly to his feet, fully awake in the blink of an eye in a way that made Christian want to slug him one. Jonah moved to the door and used one hand to work open the series of locks. His other hand, still full of Christian's seed, hung at his side. Opening the door just enough, he let Rodrigo in with a gravelly "hello." As he passed by Christian, he said, "I'll go take a shower. Give me five minutes and it's yours."

Christian couldn't look left or right without facing the eyes of men who both knew how to read him far too easily. "Yeah. Thanks." He mumbled that to the sounds of Jonah walking away and Rodrigo chuckling from just inside the door.

Right then, Abby opened the screen door and let herself in, asking, "Hey, Chris, what's up with you?"

The trifecta. His humiliation was complete.

Great.

* * *

Jonah stumbled to the bathroom and locked the door, leaning heavily on the wood once inside. He somehow remained steady as a rock in front of Christian, as well as Rodrigo for those few seconds, but inside, Jonah shook with suppressed need. He wanted Christian. He wanted the man so fucking badly, but he didn't know how in the hell to handle the raging passion or what to do about it. Jonah didn't pursue women *or* men; he just accepted what came his way when it did, and he never ached for more during the dry spell in between those partners who propositioned him.

Not anymore. Fuck. Jonah pushed his back away from the door and moved to the sink, pausing to study the too-harsh planes of his face. Every vein and pore in his body was filled with desire for Christian right in this moment; he wanted to storm right back into the living room, cover Christian right where he lay, and fuck him raw. But what did Jonah see reflected back at him in the mirror? Anger. He looked angry and like he wanted to hit someone.

He looked like a thug.

Jonah tore his gaze off his reflection with a curse, and his attention caught on the shine of Christian's cum still covering his fingers. Just looking at the glisten had Jonah curling his palm, and he swore he could still feel the burning hard length of Christian's erection singeing his hand. The springy softness of pubic hair tickled his fingertips and the satin-soft touch of Christian's heavy sac teased Jonah too, dragging a groan out of Jonah as his own cock stiffened in response once again. Christian had been so focused on his own obvious horror he hadn't noticed the hard-on straining equally big and wanting behind Jonah's zipper. The doorbell killed the physical proof of his response in a flash, but if Rodrigo hadn't shown up right then, Jonah might have done something he'd never attempted before in his life.

He might have made the first move.

Unaccustomed fear drenched Jonah just thinking about what could have happened. *He might have rejected you.* Just as his gut hit with that, Jonah focused on his hand again. *He said your name right before he came; that has to mean something.* Christ, Jonah didn't like the little talons of hope and neediness that latched onto him just thinking that Christian might find something in him worth liking. Still, his attention drifted to his shiny fingers again, and those tiny claws dug in, not letting go.

I want him.

Jonah lifted his hand in front of him. His fingers trembled as he slowly, almost against his very will, brought them to his mouth. He watched himself do it, something so purely primal it almost didn't feel human. Jonah stuck his fingers into his mouth one at a time and sucked Christian's ejaculate from his flesh, taking down the salty essence, not stopping until he dragged his tongue over his palm and cleaned every drop of leftover residue from the outside of his body and hid it on the inside. As irrational as the instinct was, Jonah didn't want anyone else to see Christian's seed or know about it.

The physical proof of Christian's excitement belonged to him, and Jonah didn't want to share.

* * *

"What do you think?" Rodrigo asked. He held up two samples of wood flooring. Next to him, Abby held one, Jonah held a few, and so did Christian. They stood in a modified circle at the local home improvement store. "I can contact my rep about any one of these styles and get it for a decent price; I just have to know which one we want so I can go ahead and put in an order for it."

With the paneling at the house finally successfully removed, the nail holes filled in, and the surfaces sanded and ready for painting over the next few days, the group started to look ahead to the next stages of work.

Jonah shifted his focus to Christian—hell, who was he kidding, it had been there already—and raised a brow. "What do you think?" he asked. Ever since the incident on the living room floor two days ago, Christian had behaved with incredible, *irritating* politeness. Jonah, flailing in the dark but unable to rein himself in, found himself prodding the man's manners every chance he got. "Which one do you like the best?"

Christian brought his gaze up to Jonah's, his eyes wide. "Me?" He shrugged. "Hell, I don't know. They're all pretty. I have nasty carpet in my apartment, so I'd kill for just about any one of them."

Squeezing his fingers so that he didn't shake Christian, much as he'd had to restrain himself when pushing the man for a preference on paint for the walls and tile for the kitchen and bathroom, Jonah shifted, blocking Rodrigo's and Abby's faces from Christian's view. "You have to have a stronger reaction to at least one over the others." Reaching back, Jonah grabbed the other samples from Rodrigo and Abby and fanned them out in his hands like playing cards. "Think of it like this: if you could afford it, and your landlord would let you do it, which one would you choose to have for yourself?"

Christian shoved the sample he held into Jonah's group too. "Why should it be up to me, *again*, Jonah?" Christian leaned in and *almost* managed to get in Jonah's face. *Finally sparking a reaction in him. About damn time.* "We're doing this as a group; we're all footing the bill. We all should have a vote and decide together."

"It looks like *I* elected you to make the choices. These two"—Jonah tried to jerk his thumb back toward Rodrigo and Abby but ended up pointing with the stack of flooring pieces in his hands—"didn't object when we were talking about the other stuff, so they damn well don't need to be in on the choice for flooring now." This time, Jonah did growl. "And don't give me that bullshit that there's not one you like more than the others; I don't believe you. This isn't a democracy; it's a home renovation, so just make a decision, Christian."

"God, I see you haven't altered your personality entirely since we were roommates as kids," Christian shot back, his face and voice full of fire. His lean, sinewy muscles strained against his black T-shirt, and he looked hotter than Jonah had ever seen him. "You can still be an incredible asshole sometimes."

"And you can still be the same pain in my ass you were back then too." Jonah buzzed with this new, incredible energy under his skin, making him wonder if he had ever been alive before this week. "What does it matter that you make the final—"

"Ladies," Rodrigo interrupted, making both men whirl on him.

Abby beat Jonah and Christian to the punch. "Hey!" She slugged Rodrigo in the arm. "That's insulting." She glared up at him. "To me, as a woman. I know how to make a decision."

"As do I," Christian said through gritted teeth. "I just don't know why my opinion should hold more weight here than all of yours."

"How about because you knew Marisol better than anyone," Abby answered. "And that even though we're helping you, it feels right that your thoughts on these things have more weight than ours."

Jonah would have grabbed Abby and kissed her smack on the mouth if he didn't think it would scare her half to death.

Christian circled his hand around Jonah's arm, making Jonah's blood rush at the touch. His eyes softening to the purest brown, Christian said, "Is that why you want me to choose everything? Because of Mari?"

No. Jonah didn't dare share his stupid-ass reason. "Will it get you to pick a floor if I say yes?"

Christian dug his hands into the pockets of his jeans. "Maybe." His lips lifted at the edge in a small smile.

"Then yes, that's why." Honesty compelled Jonah to add, "Sort of." He shifted his weight and thrust the samples right in front of Christian's face. "Damn it, will you just pick a floor already?"

Another smile, one that looked almost indulgent, crossed Christian's lips. "All right, all right. I like this one." He slid a dark wood panel from the stack. "I think it will look really rich and expensive against the neutral creams we chose for the walls."

Rodrigo snatched the sample out of Christian's hand. "Thank you. Let me make a style number note"—he already had scrap paper and a small pencil in hand—"and then we can pay for the paint. Our wood should be cut and ready; we can grab a few other things we need and get back to work."

* * *

Rodrigo lowered the tailgate of his double-cab truck and then tossed the keys to Abby, who caught them one-handed. "Open the doors and get the air going please, will you?" As Jonah was learning was Rodrigo's way, his question wasn't really a request, but an instruction. Out of the corner of his eye, Jonah saw Rodrigo's gaze slide down Abby's body, pause for a moment, but then go right back to loading planks of wood into the truck. "It's hotter than hell today," he murmured. "Careful you don't burn your legs on the seats."

One week ago, Jonah wouldn't have processed, or even picked up on, the glance Rodrigo sent Abby's way. Now, he found himself peeking looks at Christian all the time, just as Rodrigo did with Abby. Jonah stared at Christian's legs and imagined those muscular thighs clutching his waist in a firm hold as Jonah pounded Christian's ass with a furious fucking. Jonah also caught his gaze returning repeatedly to Christian's chest, where he then pictured the smooth, dark skin beneath the fabric. Jonah's lips would tingle as he wondered what Christian's skin tasted like, or if Christian's nipples would respond to licking and biting. Fuck, and then Jonah would close his eyes and feel Christian's hard cock in his hand, and his mouth would water as he relived the first taste of cum on his tongue—

"Son of a bitch." Rodrigo's curse yanked Jonah back to reality. He tore his stare off Christian and put it on Rodrigo. "We didn't get the bag with the painter's tape and the new switch plates. That was the last stuff the kid rang up. I bet he never pulled the bag off the turn after he filled it. Let me go get it. I'll be right back."

"Okay." Christian nodded at Rodrigo. "We'll have everything loaded up and ready to go by the time you get back."

As Rodrigo moved at a good clip back toward the store, Christian climbed up into the bed of the truck, helping to straighten and stack the long planks of wood they would use to resurface the porch and steps. Christian moved with comfort and ease as he strapped down the wood and secured the cans of paint with bungee cords. He leaned across to finish the task, and his T-shirt rode up, revealing the small of his back and the cuts of muscle angling down his sides to his belly. Jonah turned away, fumbling for something to do with his hands so he didn't reach out and run his fingers across the line of bronzy skin just to prove to himself that Christian was real and, yes, so was Jonah's desire for him.

"Let me give these to Abby"—Jonah snatched the handles of the leftover half dozen plastic bags of stuff—"and then I'll push these pallets to the return area so we'll be ready to go when Rodrigo gets back."

Without looking over, Christian said, "Sounds good."

Abby climbed out of the cab and took the bags from Jonah, and by the time Jonah turned around, Christian was already pushing one pallet and pulling a cart behind him, a dozen feet away. Jonah grabbed the other two pallets, employing the same push-one-pull-the-other method. Moving double time across the parking lot, he quickly caught up to Christian.

"I could have gotten those," Jonah said. He slowed down and slid into step beside Christian, right at the cart return.

"No big deal." Christian pushed his carts in first. "I have everything tied down, and we're ready to go." He stepped aside, and Jonah maneuvered his pallets into the barred holding area. "At least"—he glanced toward the store—"as soon as Rodri…"

Frissons of awareness rippled down Jonah's spine on the fade of Christian's voice. He looked to Christian, took note of the sudden tight line of the man's body and the clutch of his hands, and then followed where he stared. David walked toward them at a steady pace, one small bag folded in his left hand.

"His car wasn't parked in this area when we got here," Christian said, almost under his breath. "I would have noticed it if it was."

Son of a bitch.

"Come here." Jonah snaked his hand around Christian's neck and hauled him in against his chest. He drew in a sharp breath at the full-frontal contact, shocked at how immediately his body responded to the hard line of Christian's.

Christian reared his head back a few inches, and his focus darted all over Jonah's face. "What are you doing?" Huskiness coated Christian's voice, and Jonah's cock responded as if they rubbed up against each other without a stitch of clothing between them.

Jonah curled his other arm around Christian's waist and locked him in close. With the other, he tilted Christian's head back and started to descend. "Don't know for sure," he confessed and pressed his lips to Christian's in a soft kiss.

Their lips clung together for the briefest of moments, tantalizingly searing, and then both men jerked their heads back, their breathing instantly labored, and found each other's eyes. Caught up in Christian for a frozen moment in time, nothing else existed for Jonah except this man and Jonah's crushing need to crawl inside his very being and leave a claiming mark. The pull of desire dragged him under as nothing in his life had ever done, and Jonah yanked Christian back in, fusing their mouths together in a hard kiss with no subtlety or choreography, just a design to possess.

Jonah pried Christian's mouth open with the force of his jaw, groaning as he sank inside Christian's wet heat. He swept deeply with his tongue, meeting Christian's and tangling with equal partnership in a way that sent Jonah soaring. Never, ever, had he kissed someone like this, where he clutched hair and T-shirt with his hands and rubbed his belly and cock against another, completely aware of every part of the person he touched. *As well as how that person touches me back.* Christian kissed with equal fervor, invading Jonah's mouth and taking him over too, rushing new excitement through Jonah that left him weak in the knees.

Christian unlatched his fists from Jonah's T-shirt and slid his arms around Jonah's waist, leaning into Jonah with his weight until Jonah hit the cart railing at his back and couldn't move any farther. Without a pause, Christian slid his palms down and grabbed Jonah's ass, aggressively grinding their cocks together, both of their jeans a barrier Jonah did not want.

Pulling at Christian's shirt in the back, Jonah frantically worked to unearth the very skin he had fantasized about just moments ago. He got Christian's shirt up a few inches and delved right for his lower back, gasping at the smooth heat of Christian's bare flesh under his palm. Shocking fire radiated through Jonah and he dived down with his other hand, digging into the back of Christian's jeans to get to his ass—

Honnnkkkk. Honnnkkk.

Jonah and Christian tore apart at the blaring horn, just as a truck drove by and a guy shouted, "Get a room, assholes! This is public property!"

Jonah lunged, but Christian grabbed his arm, halting him before he took two steps. "Let him go. He's right. This isn't the place to do this." Christian straightened his shirt and wiped his mouth, still lush and full from the kiss, and looked around the half-full parking lot. His gaze narrowed, and it went from Jonah to a point in the distance, back to Jonah. "Besides"—Christian's voice wavered just a hair—"I think you made your point." He looked in the same direction of a moment ago and gestured with his shoulder. "David is a good four lanes away."

"What?" Jonah's jaw dropped. "No."

Rodrigo moved past them right then, snapping his fingers as he walked by. "I have the bag." He didn't even pause, just called out, "We're wasting daylight, guys. Let's get going."

Christian jogged to catch up to Rodrigo, without making eye contact with Jonah again or saying another word.

What the hell?

First time Jonah ever kissed someone just because he wanted to, and the guy thought it was a ruse.

Great.

Chapter Six

Jonah paced the length of the house, from the front door straight through to the back, unable to remain still, without any clue what to do about Christian. They'd worked the rest of the day with barely a dozen words between them that didn't include, "Can you hand me that roller?" or "Watch where you step." With Rodrigo and Abby right there in the house, Jonah couldn't say a damn word about what had happened in the parking lot. The kiss.

The fucking amazing kiss.

The incredible kiss that for nearly seven hours now, Christian thought happened because Jonah was trying to prove a point to that bastard David. Yet another reason for Jonah to hate the jackass.

Now it seemed like Christian did everything he could to avoid Jonah. Jonah could come up with no other explanation for Christian joining Abby for dinner when Jonah had just commented that they had leftover pizza they could eat for supper. Clearly, Christian didn't even want to be in the same house with Jonah, let alone anything more. Christ, that truth punched Jonah in the gut in a way very few things in his life ever had.

Cursing himself for ruining everything, Jonah paused at the door to their bedroom, the one room in the house—other than the bathroom—on which they had yet to do any work. As per Christian's desire to remain in the home while they worked, they would leave those spaces untouched until the end of the project. So much of this tiny bedroom looked and felt exactly the same as so many years ago, and Jonah slipped back in time to the evening that forever changed his life...

* * *

Jonah stood stock-still, stunned into paralysis by Christian's lips grinding hard against his. *What the fuck? Holy hell.* Christian had Jonah's shirt in a surprisingly tight hold, and the younger boy had his lips crushed against Jonah's in a smashing, closemouthed kiss. Jonah's heart already raced with the choices made that day, and now it squeezed with loss and guilt for this kid he knew needed a protector and friend. Jonah had patience with Christian, surprising himself by taking to this inquisitive, wiry, yet somehow athletic kid Marisol had forced him to bunk with, and he had intended to look out for Christian where he could.

Until Jonah's idiot tendencies erupted today, and he ruined everything.

Christian licked him right then and tried to push his tongue inside Jonah's mouth, and that snapped Jonah out of his fog. "No, Christian." Jonah turned his head and broke the kiss, shoving Christian away. "Fucking let go of me." He twisted his hands around Christian's and pried them out of his shirt. "You have to stop." Damn it, the kid was only fourteen years old.

"I'm sorry." Christian looked up at Jonah with big brown eyes. He held Jonah's gaze for a split second then tore it away and dropped his head down low. "You don't like me now because you know I'm a fag."

Jonah gritted his teeth. Fuck, his entire arm itched with the urge to smash his fist into the wall. "No. Damn it, Christian; don't use that word. I don't care about that." Goddamnit, he did not have time for this. The window loomed big right behind Christian's outline, but Jonah could not look past the dejected body in front of him. "You're still just a kid."

Christian snapped his focus right up off the floor, catching Jonah in the stomach with the quickness and life that always shone in it. "You're only sixteen," Christian argued right back. He grabbed for Jonah again, but Jonah snagged Christian's hands before they reached his chest. "That's not that much older than me."

"I'm a lot older in other ways." Jonah slid his eyes closed for a moment as his life caught up to him, making him weary. "You're just going to have to trust me on that."

Jonah clutched Christian's fists in order to keep them off his chest. Christian didn't fight the hold; instead, he twisted his fingers around Jonah's and ended up holding Jonah's hands. The surprisingly tight grip brought Jonah's gaze back up to Christian and had him looking into eyes that suddenly didn't seem so young. Jonah shivered, but for all his much bigger size, he couldn't pull his hands away.

Christian smiled, his lips tight. His eyes, though, Christ, the depths in his eyes frightened Jonah to his combative core. "I'm sorry you're so sad all the time," Christian said softly.

Jonah shook his head, the sudden racing in his heart having nothing to do with the stupid, irreversible choice he'd made a short while ago. "I'm not."

"Yeah, you are." Christian let go of Jonah's hands and threw himself into Jonah's arms, raising up on tiptoe and burying his face in Jonah's neck. He mumbled into Jonah's throat, "I wanted you to like me so you would tell me why you're sad and mad and don't like anybody. I wanted us to be friends, and even though I'm smaller than you I wanted to have your back and hang out with you."

You're killing daylight, man; you have to go. The window beckoned to Jonah like some giant mouth that, if he only dived in, would swallow him, and he could disappear from the planet forever. Wiry arms squeezed his waist, though, with far more strength than they should possess. And fuck, moisture dotted Jonah's skin. The wetness of another person's tears—*for him*—sank into Jonah's very marrow, crippling him where he stood.

Jonah dug his hand into Christian's hair, unearthing his face from hiding. "Listen to me." Jonah stopped for a moment, the thickness in his throat tightening his voice with emotion in a way he hadn't let happen in over two years. He gripped Christian's head, dipping down so they were at eye level. "If I'd been smart enough to have a friend, it would have been you."

Christian grasped Jonah's forearms, holding on tight. "Yeah?"

"Yeah." Light caught the pendant hanging from the chain dangling around Jonah's neck. Letting go of Christian, Jonah wrapped his hand around the infinity pendant and pulled, snapping the chain. "Here, take this. It's platinum. If you ever need some money, take it somewhere and sell it. Let it help you out."

"No." Christian shoved it back at Jonah. "It's yours."

Jonah stepped back and held up his hands. "It's yours now."

The doorbell rang, pulling both boys up short. Jonah closed his eyes, the consequence of his choice—choices— washing through him with icy cold. "I'm not gonna need it where I'm going anyway."

A light switched on in Christian's eyes, and he straightened to attention. "What are you talking about? Come on! Come on!" Christian shoved the necklace into his pocket and wrapped his hands around Jonah's arm, pulling him toward the window. "Get out of here right now. You can still get away."

"No." Jonah dug in his heels, preventing Christian from moving him another inch. He came into this room panicked, wanting to grab some stuff and run, but looking at Christian—at the flat-out, pure *goodness* in the kid— everything in Jonah calmed. A decision made, he knew he wouldn't climb out that window now for all the money in the world. He slung his bag off his shoulder and let it fall to the floor. "You're not gonna help me do this. It's time to stop."

"No, please."

"Yes." Jonah backed his way to the door and turned the knob. Opening it, Marisol's familiar tone mingled with deeper ones. Jonah didn't recognize the male voices, but he knew why the men were there. Fear drenched him in a soaking splash, but Jonah made himself look at Christian, and he overcame the desire to run. "You're a good guy, Christian," he said softly. "Don't ever let anyone tell you different." He smiled, letting it overtake his face in a way he *never* let anyone see. "It was good knowing you. Bye." Jonah pulled his stare off Christian and moved down the hall, away from the one nice thing in his life, knowing full well he walked straight into a new kind of hell.

Jonah entered the living room to Marisol's voice saying, "No, I'm certain this boy is lying to get himself out of trouble. Jonah has made mistakes, yes, but he would never do what you say. Not armed robbery. Not with a gun."

His hands already up in the air, Jonah said, "I did what they said... Ahh!" One of the officers overtook him in a flash and pushed him into the wall, holding him there with a hand clamped on his neck and an order to put his hands behind his head. Through his cheek shoved into the paneling, the pat down, and then the chilling slide of metal locking around his wrists, Jonah kept talking, before cowardice took him over and he clammed up. "I'm not gonna fight it. The money is in my front pockets, and I can take you to where I threw the gun."

In the midst of the officer reading him his rights, and Marisol frantically asking the second officer what would happen next, Jonah looked up to a sea of faces that three months ago he arrogantly proclaimed he didn't want to know. Humiliation and shame burned through him as the other kids under Marisol's care stood around the living room, staring at the scene before them in abject horror. All of them, younger than him—*Jesus, they would forever have this moment etched into their heads*—stared at Jonah, clearly terrified of what he had brought into this place of safety. Jonah felt the eyes of one other but couldn't make himself look toward the archway, where he knew Christian stood. That one, seeing the cops arrest Jonah like this, took out Jonah's legs, making him stumble as the officer hauled him toward the door.

"You're hurting him!" Christian rushed across the living room and slammed into Jonah, trying to pull him away. "He's not bad. I love him! Let him go!"

No no no. Jonah slumped, hurting and beaten inside, without any strength. Marisol swooped in at the same time as the second officer and wrapped her arms around Christian, hauling his back against her front, somehow managing to hold on to the boy who was the same height as she was.

Steeling himself, Jonah lifted his gaze to Christian's. "Kid—"

Christian jutted his chin and struggled against Marisol's hold. "I love you, Jonah."

Jonah cracked inside, but he forced familiar hardness to his face. "Don't. I don't want it." As the officer hauled Jonah through the door to the porch, Jonah looked to Marisol, pleading with more than his eyes. He did it with every strung-tight fiber in his body. "Don't let him. Please."

Jonah's last picture was Marisol nodding and turning Christian in her arms, hugging him tight. Breathing a little easier, Jonah let the police officers guide him into the backseat of the patrol car without a fight. Christian was a good, smart kid with a bright future, and Marisol would see to it that he was okay. As for himself, Jonah leaned back against the patrol car seat and closed his eyes.

Jonah knew he didn't matter.

* * *

Blinking as he came out of the memory, Jonah found himself standing on the front porch, evening light fading as darkness caught up with the hour. His palms were sweating and blood rushed fast through his system, leaving him clammy, even though the temperature still hovered around eighty degrees. Every sound, smell, and sight from that day fifteen years ago hovered in Jonah's senses, so much so it had brought him outside, walking the steps again while reliving his arrest.

He had made such a pivotal choice that day, one that changed his life.

One that saved his life too.

Pleading guilty and going into juvenile detention probably saved him from landing in a state prison for a crime that might have ended with him hurting someone, if not himself. Without JD, Jonah wouldn't have finished high school or learned to fix cars and bikes in an outreach program. He wouldn't have met Henry, the mechanic who volunteered his time in the program, who encouraged Jonah to take some college business courses, and who eventually offered Jonah a job in one of his shops when Jonah needed a place to go after his release. If he hadn't gone through JD and met Henry, Jonah wouldn't now own Henry's repair shop, and one other to go along with it. Jonah owed his very life to that one evening when he decided to turn himself in.

Which meant he owed everything to Christian.

It always came back to Christian, even though Jonah didn't know anything about the person as a man, beyond what he'd learned this week. Jonah never let Marisol tell him about Christian, and he made her swear that she would never tell Christian of her contact with him. For so much of that time, even while learning, Jonah didn't believe he would last past the age of twenty-one. He also lived with the fear that when he got out of JD, he would go right back to making stupid choices and end up in an adult prison the next time.

After his release, Jonah still hadn't learned to trust a damn soul, and possibly more insidious, he just didn't know how to be comfortable around people. Erratic homeschooling and rural isolation until his mother died had planted the seeds of inadequacy, to then playing foster home roulette for two years and, afterward, spending three years in juvenile detention grew the weed until it reached a point where Jonah knew he could not kill it. To this day, he would guess his employees didn't know a damn thing about him other than that he paid them on time and rewarded good work with financial bonuses. Jonah found money compensated very nicely for any lack of personal skills the other bosses of the world possessed that he did not.

Financial success wasn't doing Jonah a hell of a lot of good right now, where having even just a hint of social awareness might give him the answers to what to do about this turmoil Christian stirred up in him. He couldn't comprehend how or why he wanted this one person so badly. He didn't understand how it could take up so much of his thinking or how he could strip a wall and suffer a monstrous headache from the ear-bleeding scraping noise, yet still have a complete and constant awareness of where Christian was in the house, in relation to him, and who he talked and laughed with, and what he said.

For the longest time, Jonah had been proud of one thing in his life, and that was making Marisol promise to help Christian forget about his little crush. Now Jonah ached to erase that honorable act so that he could taste Christian again, and do it with so much more than just a kiss.

Groaning as he remembered, Jonah's dick pressed against his jeans with the memory of the kiss in the parking lot: the one between two fully grown, consenting men, the one his body responded to immediately in every way, as it had never done for another human being. Jonah could take another shower and jerk off to alleviate the hard-on, but he had just done that half an hour ago to relieve the half wood he'd been dealing with all day since the kiss. Fuck, he didn't like this bizarre insecurity and just wanted to go back to two weeks ago when he didn't care all that much if he said the wrong thing or made himself look indifferent or stupid.

He didn't want his peace of mind all tied up in someone else's life and choices.

Well, it is, so just deal with it or ignore it until you head back to Miami and your life gets back to normal. Ignoring this bothersome new tick sounded good to Jonah. He went back inside the house, pausing to flip on the porch light for Christian before heading to the kitchen for some leftover pizza. *You don't live in Coleman anyway; Christian is getting over a relationship, and you don't know how to be in one yourself. You're not exactly a prize, Roberts, and you know it.* Looking at the cold pizza, Jonah's stomach suddenly turned, roiling at the idea of food. Disgusted with himself, Jonah tossed the box on the counter, where it slid into something that jangled as it hit the floor. Leaning down, Jonah grabbed up a set of keys, freezing as his thumb slid over a smooth swirl of metal he hadn't felt under his fingertips in fifteen years.

His infinity pendant.

"Son of a bitch." Christian had kept it, all this time. *Damn.* Jonah's stomach flip-flopped once again, and the hum that constantly lived under his skin these days vibrated hard enough to raise the hairs on his neck and arms. His hand shook as he held up the infinity pendant Christian had turned into a key ring—an item Christian kept on his body on a daily basis. Jonah put the pendant to his lips and swore he could feel Christian's body heat still warming the precious metal. "All this time, and you never got rid of it."

The inevitable, smart or not, dragged Jonah under, urging him to move. He barely paused long enough to close and lock windows and doors before he tore out of the house and hopped on his bike, a man with a mission.

* * *

Christian knocked on the neighbor's door and stuffed his hands into his pockets. He waited on the front porch, but his gaze slid back to Mari's house, and he wondered where Jonah could have gone. The guy said he was just going to hang out and relax, and it wasn't as if Christian and Abby had to wait endlessly for service at Thomasine's, a local Cuban eatery. *Apparently, you were gone long enough.*

Hell, after the tension of the last few days and then the kiss today, Christian grudgingly admitted that Jonah might have decided a local motel was better than sharing a house and a bedroom with Christian. Goddamnit, Christian still could not believe he had shoved Jonah's hand down his pants and forced the man to help him come. Jonah was a loner with some bad stuff in his past, but he had also looked out for Christian for the brief time they were foster brothers, so Christian knew the man had great kindness and a warrior's instinct in him. The whole situation with David brought Jonah's protective instincts raging to the surface, so much so they were blurring all kinds of lines between them that might be better served remaining clear.

The door in front of him swung open. "Christian!" Ida, Marisol's longtime neighbor, smiled big and wide. "My, you get more handsome every day." She clapped his shoulders like a linebacker psyching up a teammate for a play. "What can I do for you?"

"I need to borrow your spare key for Mari's house." Christian shifted and waved to Abby, letting her know it was okay to head home. "I left mine inside, and Jonah's not there to let me in."

"Oh, he just left a few minutes ago," Ida shared. She continued to chat as she left Christian at the door and moved through her house. "I was washing dishes and saw him walk that big motorcycle of his past my window. He waits until he gets that machine to the street before he turns it on, and I do appreciate that. My goodness, starting that thing right by the window might give my poor heart some problems." Ida appeared at the end of the long hallway and waddled on short legs back to the front door. "Here you go." She handed over a single key on a ring with a butterfly attached. "Bring it back tomorrow, and I will keep it until you finish fixing up the house. Okay?"

"Will do, ma'am. Thank you." Christian leaned down and pecked a kiss on her full cheek. "Good night." Christian loped down the stairs and jogged across the yard, up his porch steps, and waved to Ida where she watched him from her porch. He let himself inside and opened the living room windows a few inches each, letting in air to help dissipate the smell of paint. Moving into the bedrooms to do the same, his attention caught on Jonah's duffel bag on the floor at the foot of his bed, and his heart started to hammer.

He didn't move out.

Christian's legs turned to jelly, making him unsteady as he headed to the bathroom for a shower, mentally replaying his actions of earlier in the day. Acting like a total coward, Christian had jumped on Abby's offer of dinner and didn't even stop to wash more than his hands and face before leaving with her. Thomasine's was a casual place that catered more to call-in and pick-up orders than an actual sit-down restaurant, but Christian knew he had accepted Abby's invitation to eat out because he was afraid to be alone with Jonah. He had already put the man's hand on his dick, and he'd thrown himself into that kiss in the parking lot with total abandon too. God only knew what he might do alone in this house with Jonah tonight.

Stepping in the shower, Christian stuck his head under the water and let the warm flow soak his hair and trickle down his body. He shampooed and soaped up quickly, gritting his teeth and ordering his body not to respond as he cleaned his cock, balls, and ass. Just touching his pucker drew a quiver through his channel, reminding him how much he liked his asshole penetrated and stuffed full with another man's cock, or even a toy a partner used to torment him. God, it had been forever since experiencing either one of those things, and Christian ached for the contact that came with being in an intimate relationship. His chute craved the invasion, and Christian imagined Jonah's penis— all hard and thick and long—pushing its way past the barrier of Christian's ring. Christian pushed at his entrance with two fingers—

Christian whipped his hand away, horrified at his inability to control himself. Standing under the spray, Christian rinsed himself off quickly, eager to get to bed and fall asleep before Jonah came back home. He could not lie awake across from Jonah with that kiss still front and center in his mind, tormenting him with this childhood crush come to full fruition in his adult life, and not have his eagerness and need show in his eyes. Better to avoid the man for a few days until he could get these revived feelings back under control. Even better than that? Get Marisol's house renovated in record time and get Jonah on the road back home.

Coward. Christian growled at himself as he turned off the water and stepped out of the shower, grabbing a towel and wrapping it around his waist. He studied himself long and hard in the mirror while brushing his teeth, wondering when in the hell he had become this person. This person too scared to own what he wanted. This person who worried about one man's opinion so deeply that he became a different person than Marisol taught him to be. This person who intended to run from the bathroom to his bed and hide under the covers, who wouldn't even finger-fuck himself out of fear of the face he would see in his mind or the name he would shout as he came.

This person who hid a teenage attraction that had never gone away.

Disgusted with himself, Christian spit toothpaste, rinsed his mouth, and wiped his face. He didn't like this guy in the mirror very much right now, and he turned away, swearing at his behavior today. Jonah had done nothing to warrant Christian running out on him so fast that he hadn't even taken the time to grab his fucking keys. Christian *never* forgot his keys.

He didn't dare risk losing Jonah's pendant.

Christian turned back to the mirror, staring until he saw past his eyes straight into his soul. He refused to look away as his image blurred; he gripped the edge of the sink, sweating his way through the cowardly instinct to hide. He didn't blink until he knew he would sit up all night if necessary, waiting for Jonah. He would apologize for the cold shoulder treatment today and keep doing it until Jonah believed him.

Taking a deep breath, Christian steadied his nerves, opened the bathroom door, and ran smack into Jonah's immovable force.

"Oh," Christian blurted, "hi."

Jonah stood tall and big, fierce, and wound up tight, and goddamnit, he made Christian almost forget his own name. Jonah stepped forward, and Christian stepped back, moving into the wave of humid air still overtaking the bathroom.

Jonah opened his mouth, made a strange noise, and then closed it and looked down and away, swearing a litany under his breath.

Unable to break away from the powerful draw, Christian stepped closer and cupped Jonah's jaw, snapping the man's wild gaze off the floor. Christian tried to smile, although he wasn't sure he quite made the transition. "You okay?" he asked, keeping his voice gentle.

"No. Yes." Roughness tore up Jonah's voice, the sound touching Christian like a sandpaper caress. Jonah cursed again but this time grabbed Christian's face and forced it up to his. "I didn't kiss you because of him." He scraped his mouth across Christian's, and Christian felt a shudder go through the bigger man as he did it. "I didn't kiss you because of him," he said again, snagging their lips together one more time. "I promise."

With that, Jonah skimmed his callused hands down Christian's damp torso to his belly and released the loose knot of the towel around Christian's waist, letting it fall to a heap on the floor.

Chapter Seven

Christian inhaled sharply and took a step back. The one small move crushed Jonah right where he stood. Jonah looked away, caught his darting gaze in the mirror, and dropped it lower, unable to look at himself as his stomach plummeted right to the floor.

Shit, shit, shit. Say something, Roberts. You just tore off Christian's towel. You gave yourself away; there's no turning back now.

"I want you." Jonah's esophagus rubbed raw as he forced out that one short sentence. His head averted, eyes focused on the sink, Jonah clutched Christian's bare hip in one hand and a small paper bag in the other. He let go of Christian in a shot and thrust the bag in the man's face. "I went out and bought stuff." Just as quickly as he shoved the bag of condoms and lube at Christian, Jonah hid it behind his back. His mouth, unfortunately, kept right on going. "We kissed, and I liked it. In the parking lot, I mean. The first time you were too young, but this time you weren't. And maybe I shouldn't like it or want more from you, because you were a good kid and you've become a fine man, and I was right to tell Marisol to make you forget me, even though I never forgot you. And I thought you did let go, but then you forgot your keys, and I knocked them to the floor and saw the pendant, and I got so fucking hard... Shit, I was already hard, but I got harder, and I knew I wanted you, and I left to go get stuff because I didn't have anything and I didn't know if you did. Maybe you don't even want me back in the same way, even if you did have stuff. But you did say my name, and Christ, it felt so fucking good when you came in my ha—"

Christian grabbed Jonah's hand, shoved it down over his cock, and very efficiently found the one way to shut Jonah up. Like the other morning, Christian covered Jonah's hand and helped him find the right stroke, hissing and jerking when Jonah took over the task. Christian's visible response pulled an answering one out of Jonah, stiffening his prick to the point where it pressed painfully against his jeans.

"Oh yeah." Christian rocked into Jonan's rubbing. "Just like that." Leaning into Jonah's body, Christian lifted on his toes until his mouth grazed Jonah's ear. "Look at me." He grinned against Jonah's neck; Jonah could feel it. Just as quickly, Christian nipped Jonah's flesh. He then took Jonah's belt buckle in hand, working it out of the loop. "Look me in the eyes, Jonah"—he undid Jonah's button and slid his zipper down—"so I can say yes."

Groaning with need, Jonah turned his head and dipped down, searching for Christian's lips. His cheek grazed Christian's damp hair and rubbed over his temple and face. He finally found Christian's mouth and stole a biting kiss. Deepening the kiss, Jonah forced Christian's lips apart, and Christian relented, accepting the rudimentary, overeager invasion of Jonah's tongue. He even kissed Jonah back, holding him inside with suction on his tongue. Jonah's legs nearly buckled, and he grabbed Christian around the waist, hauling him in, nearly as much to give Jonah support as to get Christian as close as possible in every single way.

Jonah ran his hands down the base of Christian's back and cupped his bare ass, letting the smooth, firm flesh singe his palms and set him on fire. He slid his fingers into Christian's tight crease and grazed the man's hole. He had never touched another person's ass in such a way, but fuck, he already craved something more intimate. He wanted inside.

"Jesus." Breaking the kiss, panting to regain his breath, Jonah rubbed the tip of his pointer finger over the striated entrance again. At the same time, he licked Christian's lower lip. "You feel as good as you taste."

Christian nibbled back on Jonah's sensitized lips, and damn if Jonah couldn't feel another small smile as he did it. "I just brushed my teeth." Christian pulled at the hem of Jonah's T-shirt and grazed his palms over Jonah's stomach and chest as he pushed the fabric up, making Jonah shiver at the contact. "Everything is minty fresh."

"No, it's not the toothpaste." Jonah lifted his arms and let Christian remove his shirt. The material swept over his head and fell to the floor, and Jonah found Christian's gaze again. His voice gruff, he added, "It's you."

Light sparked in Christian's eyes, turning them to the darkest chocolate. "God, man. The things you say... Damn it"—he stepped back—"look at what you do to me."

Almost afraid, Jonah took his first full viewing of Christian's naked body, and it stole his very breath away.

Dark tan skin pulled tightly over sinewy lines of muscle owed to Christian's athletic background, a fitness he clearly maintained beyond his retirement from professional baseball. A smooth chest with tiny brown nipples gave way to a tapered, flat stomach, lightly hairy thighs, and big feet.

His mouth dry as a bone, Jonah's gaze traveled back up Christian's legs, and he finally let himself stare openly at Christian's prick: long, hard, and pointing north from within a tamed patch of dark hair. Jonah's throat went from desert dry to full of saliva in a flash, just from looking at Christian's erection. His own cock pushed equally fiercely, free from the confinement of zipped jeans but still trapped behind his underwear. Christian's body posed a virtual smorgasbord of places Jonah wanted to stop and feast, but one overwhelming need hit him harder than all the rest. *I want my mouth full of his cock.*

"I've never hungered for someone before." Jonah dropped to his knees on that confession. He felt almost as if he worshipped at the altar of another person's body. More than that, his entire being responded to the almost-submissive thought, growing tight with the desire to possess and to be owned equally so. Christian's stomach muscles quivered in front of Jonah, and a thick bead of precum grew on the tip of his cock, teasing Jonah's newly unearthed needs. "But I can't seem to stop wanting when it comes to you."

"Shit, Jonah..." Christian dug his fingers into Jonah's hair and forced his face up. Jonah found dark eyes waiting for him, and he swore to God they saw past the confusion, defensiveness, and awkwardness, straight into the truth in

Jonah's soul, struggling to show itself to this one person. "The things you say."

Growling, panicked with this vulnerability, Jonah buried his face in Christian's crotch, hiding and taking at the same time. He inhaled deeply, and the clean fragrance of soap and musky scent of man that could never be washed away filled Jonah's nostrils, rushing through his system faster than the purest alcohol and intoxicating him as quickly. Christian's hard, hot cock seared a burn mark into Jonah's right cheek, enticing Jonah to turn his head and lick a line from base to tip and then engulf the dark head when taste testing wasn't enough.

"Oh, shit yeah..." Christian bucked in front of him and inadvertently shoved more of his dick into Jonah's mouth. "More. Fuck, take more."

Jonah eagerly opened wider and did as asked, forcing nearly half of Christian's cock past his lips. Salt, heat, and man burst on Jonah's tongue, popping every taste bud and nerve ending in his mouth to excited life. He dug his fingers into Christian's ass, holding him in place as he bobbed up and down Christian's shaft, lapping and licking and sucking, anything that would give him more of Christian. Jonah didn't know if he should move over Christian's flesh or stay where he was in order to give Christian the most joy. For Jonah, he just wanted everything, all at the same time, so he sucked down Christian's cock, only to drag all the way back up with a vacuum of tightness, and then take as much as he could back inside again.

Rumbling noises of pleasure escaped Christian and spun through Jonah, making him dizzy. He didn't know anything about giving anyone else pleasure, but every sound Christian made, and every time Christian pumped his hips into Jonah's face with a little grinding motion, Jonah grew increasingly excited and wanted to do more, give more, make Christian *feel* more, anything that would help tie them together when they were apart.

Apart. No, please. Jonah's insides seized, and he doubled his efforts, suddenly almost panicked to make Christian come. He held Christian to him with a rough grip, one ass cheek clutched so tightly in each hand that he split Christian open in the back and inadvertently slipped his middle finger over Christian's snug ring, filling Jonah with an aching desire to push through the snapped-shut bud. Jonah's cock pounded with its own heartbeat in time with Christian's, and he could think of nothing more perfect than getting inside Christian's tight ass.

Christian thrust back into Jonah's blunt fingertip and circled his tight pucker against the pad. "Ah, God, yeah, I'm throbbing inside for you." Christian reached back, pried Jonah's hand off his ass, and brought it to Jonah's face. "Wet it, wet it." Christian didn't wait for Jonah to help; he forced two of Jonah's fingers into Jonah's mouth next to Christian's cock, stretching Jonah's lips and jaw open even wider. Christian braced his free hand against the wall, hissing as he looked down at Jonah, cock and fingers shoved in his mouth. "God, you're the fucking sexist thing I've ever seen. Wet your fingers. I want you in my ass."

Stuffed full, almost to the point of discomfort, Jonah had never felt more primal and sexual. He laved at his own fingers, tasting the saltiness of sweat and rich male musk. He somehow rolled his tongue around everything invading his mouth, slicking his fingers and Christian's erection with so much saliva that it dripped down the corner of his mouth.

Right then, Christian uttered, "Oh fuck, that's good. Need you." He dragged Jonah's fingers back out, pushing them into the split of his ass again, and Jonah no longer cared about the picture he made. He had Christian's cock taking over his mouth and his fingers against Christian's asshole, with Christian *holding* his hand there. For the first time in his life, Jonah thought he found the person hiding inside him; he knew who he was supposed to be.

Christian's man.

Jonah shuddered, frightened to his core by the certainty of that thought living in his soul. Needing to hide, Jonah drove his middle finger through Christian's sphincter and shoved his way home, breaching that tight barrier and invading the scorching channel on the other side.

"Ahh! Fuck...fuck..." Christian's asshole squeezed down on Jonah's finger, sucking half of it inside, where Christian's rectum immediately started rippling all around Jonah's digit in shivery spasms.

Instinct and the need to claim ownership took Jonah over completely, and he quickly started finger-fucking Christian's ass in time with every suck on his cock, overwhelmed by the desire to bring Christian to his knees with pleasure. When Jonah pulled off Christian's cock, he pushed his finger inside Christian's ass, taking him until he could go no farther, and then pulled out his finger only to bob back in on Christian's dick, letting Christian's rigid thickness overtake his mouth again. Soon it wasn't enough, and Jonah worked a second finger through Christian's stretched ring. Christian whimpered in response, and Jonah's own ass channel pulsed, shocking him with equal wanting. The thrill of thinking Christian would take his body in this same way rocked through Jonah at full force, and he redoubled his fucking efforts, sawing in and out faster, imagining that Christian did the exact thing to his ass.

Jonah rubbed over a raised bump inside Christian, and the man rose up onto his toes and slammed his hand over Jonah's fingers buried in his ass. "Don't stop." Christian frantically tried to guide Jonah's fingers in and out of his anus, while simultaneously grinding his backside into the fucking. "Oh God. So close...so close... Please don't ever stop."

Jonah tried to mumble, "Won't," but didn't want to release Christian's prick for even the second it would take to say the word. Christian pumped his hips furiously at Jonah's face and continued to hold Jonah's digits inside his rectum. His eyes glazed over and his mouth fell open, as if he struggled to take everything Jonah did to him. The sight of Christian was a picture of pure beauty to Jonah, but it wasn't enough. He needed more. He needed everything.

He needed Christian to lose all control.

Unsure, but unable to stop, Jonah breathed through his nose and loosened his jaw as much as he could, and this time when he went down on Christian's cock, he kept right on going, struggling, but pushing the tip past his throat. At the same time, he forced a third finger into Christian's tight ass and took him to the hilt.

Christian doubled over and sank his fingers straight into Jonah's scalp, digging deep. "Ohhhhh, shhhhittt…" His entire body jolted, his chute clamped down hard on Jonah's fingers, and he moaned long and low in his throat, spewing ejaculate as he lost the battle and came. It seemed orgasm overtook Christian's entire being; he filled Jonah's throat with his hot essence, so much that it backwashed into Jonah's mouth, where the bitter flavor covered Jonah's tongue, cheeks, and even his teeth, tagging Jonah with ownership that he never knew he wanted.

Another shiver washed over Jonah, devastating in its chill. The tightness grabbed at his chest, pushing him to aggression and the need to dominate; to prove he could mark Christian even more completely than Christian did to him.

Jonah withdrew his fingers from Christian's ass, pulled off his softening cock in a flash, and spun the guy around. He chopped out Christian's knees, took him to the floor, and immediately covered him completely, his much-bigger body pushing Christian into the cool linoleum. Jonah shoved one hand in between their bodies and yanked his cock out of his underwear, and with the other, he grabbed the drugstore bag, shook it open, and spilled its contents onto the floor. "I don't want a condom." He snatched up the lube and put the cap to his teeth, breaking the protective seal and popping the lid. Messy, too frantic to make his fingers work steadily, Jonah shoved the tube of lube between their bodies and squeezed, coating Christian's crease with the thick substance. Jonah worked the lube inside Christian's ass, groaning as his fingers were encased in Christian's snug heat again. Damn it, Jonah's cock reared against the back of his hand, so fucking eager to feel that inferno too. "Condom." The word came out low, little more than a grunting order. "Tell me if I need it."

Christian lifted his ass into the touch, driving Jonah crazy. Moaning, Christian bore his cheek into the flooring and pushed his back and buttocks up into Jonah's front. "Good if you are."

Jesus fucking Christ. Jonah uttered, "Good too," moved his hand, and drove his cock deep into Christian's ass.

Christian cried out and bucked into the invasion and somehow helped slip Jonah's length even farther inside his body.

"Tight, Christian… You're so fucking tight." Blinding, white-hot pleasure consumed Jonah, clamping a stranglehold on his dick that took him over completely. He dropped down on top of Christian, fusing chest to back, and pushed Christian's body into the floor with every hard, uncontrollable thrust of his cock into Christian's tight ass. Each shove slid Christian under him, making Jonah growl at even the slightest separation of the rudimentary mating. He dug his hands under Christian's armpits and wrapped himself around Christian's shoulders, anchoring the man as he pounded Christian's passage in rapid strokes, needing the heat, the friction, the very *act*, like he needed to breathe.

"Oh…ahh"—red suffused Christian's cheek and neck, and he inhaled sharply—"so fucking big." He reached his arms out and planted his palms against the side of the bathtub, helping give Jonah an unmovable body to fuck.

Shame at his aggressive taking attacked Jonah's conscience, and every grunt Christian made with each plow into his ass filled Jonah with rage, directed at himself, but none of that could make him slow down or stop. He buried his face in Christian's hair, furrowing through the thick, clean-smelling stuff until he reached Christian's ear. He licked and bit, without gentleness. Christ, it was another opening, and unable to help himself, Jonah thrust his tongue inside, taking Christian's ear with the same force and pace he used to fuck the man's snug ass.

Christian squeezed his eyes shut and gritted his teeth, and Jonah had never felt more like an animal. "Sorry." Even as the one stripped-down word slipped out, Jonah pulled his cock all the way out of Christian's channel so that he could slam it all the way home again. Claiming Christian consumed Jonah with every single raw act he had ever dreamed in his life, only to eventually suppress as unnatural thoughts. Purely base desires rushed through Jonah, ones that made him want to spray his seed all over Christian's body; it rivaled the need to empty a load in Christian's ass. Jonah felt certain Christian could see the dehumanizing thoughts and feelings living inside him, yet even Christian's horror and eventual rejection couldn't make Jonah loosen his hold on Christian's shoulders that would surely leave bruises, let alone lift his suffocating weight or slow the rough fucking. He could only say, "I'm sorry, I'm sorry, I'm sorry," into Christian's ear, again and again, with every deep ramming of the other man's quivering anus.

Opening his eyes, Christian turned his head, and somehow found Jonah's gaze. "No sorrys...ahhh, fuck!" He winced, but the burn in his eyes never broke from Jonah's. Christian somehow spread his legs and hooked his feet around the backs of Jonah's knees, locking them together in a crazy tangle of limbs. "Don't stop." He strained his neck and captured Jonah's mouth in a clinging kiss, drawing a shudder and then a complete, sudden stillness in Jonah. "I want it," Christian shared. He darted his tongue against the seam of Jonah's lips, the move so teasing and gentle it scared the shit out of Jonah. Christian rubbed his mouth over Jonah's jaw, cheek, and temple, and finally whispered at his ear, "I want you."

"Oh-oh…" Jonah's mouth fell open as the endgame rushed over him, no way to hold it back at all. "Ohhh, fuck." Everything swirling within him burst out in sudden, complete, deep waves of quiet orgasm, a release unlike anything he had ever experienced. Closing his eyes as it happened, Jonah wanted to fight the sense of complete exposure that made him feel naked and open in every way, but he couldn't move a muscle. He could only be still and experience the moment. No tightening in his balls or sense of swelling in his cock, Jonah simply spilled deep inside Christian's body, emptying his seed in a continuous, hot stream, giving Christian something he had never given another soul on this planet. A piece of his very being.

And he didn't mean his cum.

The vulnerability knocked the wind right out of Jonah, and he collapsed on Christian's back.

"Jonah." Christian gasped under him, snapping Jonah's eyes open and putting his mind and body back into the bathroom—where he crushed Christian into the floor with his weight.

Jonah yanked off Christian in a heartbeat and stumbled into the wall, quickly pulling his underwear and jeans back up to his waist. His feet rooted in place, he felt nailed to the wallpaper by Christian's dark, unwavering stare.

Oh, shit. I fucked him. Jonah couldn't move his legs. *What in the hell am I supposed to say and do now?*

Chapter Eight

Christian stared at Jonah and felt like an eighteen-wheeler bearing down on a buck standing in the middle of the highway, with Jonah playing the deer frozen in Christian's headlights. Jonah stood so very still, his body so big, everything in him clearly radiating that he wanted to look small and disappear into the flower-patterned wallpaper behind him. Lying on the floor of Mari's bathroom, Christian's mind raced with thought after thought about the best way to deal with a man like Jonah Roberts.

Play hardball, Sanchez; the guy won't respect a pussy.

Christian rolled over and got his feet under him, groaning at how quickly stiffness set in when using a cold floor as a bed. As he stood, his sore ass reminded him that he hadn't been down on the linoleum alone.

Jonah cleared his throat, cutting through the thick silence first. "I was rough with you." He held Christian's gaze in the laser of his pale one but then glanced away. "I apologize for my aggression."

The gravel layering Jonah's tone had Christian taking a tentative step forward, *almost* into Jonah's personal space. Every stance, every abrupt word, every uncomfortable rough edge in this man rang new bells of insight in Christian's mind, making his heart hurt.

Studying Jonah in this new light, Christian said, "You're afraid, aren't you?"

Jonah reared back, slid a fleeting look Christian's way, but didn't calm or focus on him. "What?"

Bracing his hands on the wall on either side of Jonah, Christian obliterated Jonah's invisible zone of protection. Jonah's pupils flared, but Christian refused to back away. "You're scared of something, Jonah; every line in your body gives you away." Jonah had a lot of bulk and inches on Christian, but right now, the bigger man emanated the need for protection in forceful, tangible waves. "Is it that you admitted you want another man, and you've never felt that before, so you don't know how to deal with it? Maybe you aren't sure you even want to deal with it? Is it just the fact that you want someone in general and don't like feeling that way?"

Swearing, Jonah somehow managed to fuse his back even more completely to the wall. "For Christ's sake, Christian. No, it's not any of that crap." Jonah kept darting in and out of eye contact with Christian, not allowing Christian to get any kind of deeper read on him. "It's nothing."

Christian had dealt with enough mixed signals in his relationship with David, and he *would not* get caught in the middle of someone else's sexual confusion or denial again. "So then maybe you just needed a quick fuck to release some tension, and now you don't know how to tell me to get los—"

Jonah snaked his hand around Christian's neck and pulled him close, his eyes harkening a storm. "Don't say shit like that." He crushed his mouth down on Christian's, violent and hard, bruising Christian's lips. He strong-armed Christian and thrust him away just as fast as he pulled him in. He moved through the open bathroom door but paused on the other side and pointed back in at Christian. "You're nobody's quick fuck. Don't ever say that." He curled his hand into a fist. "Just...don't."

Jonah took another step, but Christian leaped and grabbed Jonah's hand before he could get away. "Then what is it?" he pleaded. "Tell me."

The tight fist locked under Christian's grip fairly vibrated, as did the man in front of him. Jonah's jaw ticked visibly, and he looked for all the world like someone had just kicked him in the teeth, and he had no way to fight back. Jonah finally blurted, his voice raw, "It's you, damn it. Christ, Christian"—Jonah's lips paled and thinned down to almost nothing—"it's you, okay."

Every molecule of air felt sucked right out of the room, and Christian's hand fell dead to his side. "What?"

"Damn it." Jonah strode through the house, eating up the linoleum and carpet with his long legs. "I don't know what the fuck I'm doing here." He reached the front door and turned, looking all the way down the shotgun hallway to where Christian still stood at the back of the small house. His voice dropped, but Christian heard every single word, every deep breath, clear as digital. "I want you to like me, Christian, and I've fucking never cared what someone thought about me before. At least, not enough to be embarrassed that I don't have one goddamned relationship to point to and say, 'See, this person knows me and likes me, so I must be a stand-up guy.' It has never bothered me that I've never had a girlfriend, or even a boyfriend, so I don't have any idea how to be with someone, or even if I'm capable of it. I've never given a rat's ass that all the people in my life are acquaintances or employees, because I've never once in my life connected to anyone I wanted to impress and think of as a friend. I don't have a friend." His chest heaved. "Not one."

Pain clamped a tight band on Christian's heart, and he took a step forward. "Jonah."

"No." Jonah raised his hands and put up the stop sign. "You pushed this, goddamnit, so let me just get it all out. Shit, you pushed it before tonight. You've had me tied up in knots from the second I stepped over the threshold of this house, making me question myself and why I'm defective in this way"—Jonah's voice caught, and Christian started running—"and how the hell I can hide it from you so that you like me."

Christian slammed into Jonah and wrapped him up in a tight embrace. "Shh, shh." He stood on tiptoe, still naked, and rained kisses all over Jonah's unforgiving face. "I already like you, Jonah. I like you so fucking much. You don't have to be someone else for me."

Jonah manacled his arms around Christian and lifted him right off the floor. "Jesus, Christian, I don't know how to be something normal with you." His entire body shook, sending tremors into Christian. Jonah held Christian against his chest with one arm and brushed his knuckles against Christian's cheek and temple with the other. His face still looked hard and tough as hell, but his eyes were finally open in every way, showing the much different man living inside. "I just know I want you again."

Aching, Christian ran his fingers along the edge of Jonah's hair, loving the thick, dark stuff. He held Jonah's gaze, lost in its pale depths. "You can have me." Christian leaned in and laid his forehead against Jonah's, and at the same time twined his legs around Jonah's waist. "Take me to bed, Jonah, and have me right now."

A rumble started in Jonah's chest, ending in a textured growl. He swooped his mouth down, fusing his lips to Christian's as he started to walk. Christian held on tight and kissed Jonah back with everything in him, his entire body reigniting with one touch of their tongues. Jonah didn't seem to have a middle ground; he just went full out with deep, exploring kisses that were wet, messy, and raw—full of an honesty that raced through Christian's blood, had his cock hard, and his ass clenching for another fucking he knew would leave him tender tomorrow. He didn't care. Right now, nothing mattered more than getting Jonah inside him again.

Clinging and kissing, their tongues in a frantic dance, Jonah kicked at the half-closed door and stumbled inside their bedroom, letting go with one arm long enough to yank the mattress from his bed to the floor. He lowered Christian to the padding and came down on top of him in a push-up stance. Almost smiling, his face suffused with a rosy red, he said, "Frame might break with two of us. Better not to risk it."

Every nerve ending in Christian's body sparked with the memory of Jonah's recent sexual enthusiasm. The man did like to pound away on his partner. "Right." A child's bed would not withstand Jonah's particular brand of fucking.

"Damn it"—Jonah pushed up to his knees—"we need the lube."

Christian grabbed Jonah's arms and pulled him back down, toppling the man fully on top of him. "No." He spread his legs and reached down between them, fingering his slicked-up asshole. His bud already squeezed for a second penetration. "There's still enough there. You were plenty generous before."

"Sorry." Jonah spoke a foul word under his breath, looking downright stricken. "I didn't know how to slow down before, and I just dumped a bunch of the stuff onto you so I could get inside."

Folding his arms at his sides, Christian leaned up on his elbows and brushed his lips against the hard set of Jonah's. "Stop apologizing." He held Jonah's intense stare, flicked his tongue against Jonah's seam, and then darted inside for another drugging taste. Jonah's pupils flared and he moved in fast, capturing Christian's tongue and sucking hard. Christian moaned, and his dick leaked a lake of precum as he thought about that incredible blowjob Jonah had delivered, no shyness or hesitation at all.

Getting hotter than hell all over again, Christian lifted his hips and rubbed, cursing some himself when he couldn't get skin-to-skin contact. Christian bit at Jonah's lips but dropped his head back down to the mattress and sighed, breaking the kiss. Jonah growled and followed him, taking his mouth again, sweeping deeply, while at the same time rocking his jean-covered erection against Christian's perineum, and driving Christian's sweet spot wild. Christian fucking needed to feel Jonah's cock against his, *right now.*

"Damn it, Jonah." Christian dug between them for a button and zipper and started working Jonah's pants open. "Take your damn jeans off before I rip you out of them."

Jonah actually chuckled, and Christian's breath caught. God, he didn't think he had ever heard a more beautiful sound than Jonah's laugh. Jonah buried his face in the crook of Christian's neck, his big body shaking, and Christian mumbled, "I wasn't kidding, you know. I want both of us naked this time." He slid his hands in the waistband of Jonah's jeans and underwear and pushed them down his hips, freeing his dick.

Bare cock grazed bare cock, searing in its heat. Jonah hissed and rolled into the touch. "Shit." He bit Christian's shoulder and then drew up, finding his eyes again. "I was trying to keep a barrier between us to help me go slow."

Christian abandoned Jonah's jeans and shoved his hands between their bodies, wrapping up their cocks in a two-fisted glove. Burning heat slid against burning heat, scorching Christian's palms. He didn't back off one bit, though, and began working them both over with firm, long strokes, both lengths a combination of slick and sticky with lube, semen, and new precum.

The men started breathing heavier and pumping their hips, working their erections against one another, in and out of Christian's tight hold. Every touch of his fingers over the firm thickness of Jonah's prick had Christian's channel pulsing with the need for Jonah to fill him again. "Slow is overrated," Christian said heatedly. "Fuck me, Jonah"—he squeezed his thighs against Jonah's hips—"so I know it wasn't another dream."

"Jesus." Jonah looked away for a second, and Christian thought he heard the man counting to ten. Jonah shook his head and came back to Christian, no less fire shining his eyes. "You know how to get me to the end with barely a look and a word. I don't think I'm gonna last any longer this time than I did the last. Let go of me for a minute." He batted Christian's hands away and shifted, reaching down his legs. "I want my clothes off too."

He had sneakers and socks to work off in addition to the jeans, but in short order, he moved back in between Christian's thighs and settled in close, all kinds of newly naked flesh touching and rubbing, ratcheting the intimacy up a hundred notches. "Mmm..." Jonah wrapped Christian's legs around the backs of his thighs, and his eyelids slid closed as he ran his palms up and down the outer lengths, drawing goose bumps with the casual touch. "That feels nice." His cock rode the split of Christian's ass, back and forth, and then again. The long, thick length slid through the leftover lube, heating Christian's sensitive skin and tormenting his pucker with fleeting glances of Jonah's dick, but nothing more. "Shit." Jonah rocked into Christian again, making Christian's prick so damn hard. "That feels even nicer."

Christian gasped as his sphincter quivered with another light touch from Jonah's cock, driving his chute crazy as it milked and squeezed, grasping for something, anything, from Jonah.

"You don't know how to tease or go slow, my ass, Roberts." Christian glared, his body strung tight with need. Gritting his teeth, he took his own erection in hand and started to pull with a less-than-gentle drag, just as he wanted Jonah to do.

Jonah immediately settled more completely on Christian, sandwiching Christian's hand and erection between their stomachs. "It is your ass, isn't it?" As Jonah held himself up with one arm beside Christian's head, he reached between their bodies with the other and rubbed his fingers through Christian's crease, repeating the pattern he had taken with his cock. "It's a fucking incredible ass." With one bit of pressure against Christian's entrance, just enough to whet Christian's appetite for more but not break through, Jonah shifted his thighs apart, pushed Christian open higher and wider, and fit his penis to Christian's hole. "I like it a lot." He bore down on Christian's anus with the head of his cock, applying mind-blowing, exquisite force, pushing at Christian's tight ring repeatedly. Finally, with a grunt, Jonah broke through and penetrated Christian's ass. "Jesus, man"— Jonah's skin pulled taut over his face as he pushed his way deep, stretching and filling Christian's channel to the brim— "I like your ass a whole hell of a lot." He dropped down on top of Christian, wrapped his arms around Christian's head, put their faces blurrily close, and started to pump his hips, fucking Christian in steady, easy strokes.

Jonah's renewed control turned Christian's ass into a rippling tunnel of need. Christian tried to move his hips in counterbalance to Jonah's and create more friction, but Jonah quickly reached down and grabbed Christian's hip to halt him, in full command of the encounter.

"Stay still for a minute, honey," Jonah murmured. He dipped down and licked Christian's passion-swollen lips, but pulled away before Christian could grab his tongue for a deeper kiss.

Wait. He called me honey. Christian bucked as Jonah's small endearment hit him in the heart, tangling him even more messily with this man. He lunged and captured Jonah's mouth in a searing kiss, voracious and needy, trying to say something with action that he knew would freak Jonah out to hear in words. A rough noise escaped Jonah, and he slanted his mouth over Christian's in a base, aggressive kiss, eating and licking at Christian in that uncensored way Christian so loved.

Jonah thrust his tongue deep but then uttered a harsh, "no," and tore his mouth away. With heavy breaths, Jonah washed delicious heat over Christian's mouth and lips. His eyes slate and piercing, Jonah squeezed Christian's hip and curled his fingers around to Christian's buttocks, taking a cheek in hand. "I had to learn patience and how to master myself when I went away. Give me a chance to use it here with you." Jonah withdrew his dick from Christian's rectum torturously slowly and then pushed in again. He shifted his angle and somehow took Christian's ass just a little bit more.

Christian bit his lip, struggling to accept Jonah's claiming. His passage flared and fluttered with the contact, and his entrance pulled on Jonah's bigger size, something he had never taken until tonight. Jonah dragged his cock all the way out and slid back in, eliciting a moan as he pushed through Christian's opening and rubbed up against every nerve ending in Christian's chute, producing enough exquisite pleasure to make his toes curl. Christian's cock reared in response, pushing against Jonah's stomach, greedy for something from Jonah too.

"Please, Jonah." Everything felt so damn good, Christian though he might split apart inside. "You don't need to exhibit patience with me." He slid his hands up and down Jonah's sides, marveling with dizzying awareness at the heat and hardness of muscle flexing and releasing under Jonah's skin. Not stopping, Christian reached around to Jonah's wide back and ran his palms down his spine, and kept right on going until he clutched Jonah's tight ass in his hands. "We can go slow another time." He dug his fingers into Jonah's flesh, holding the man's cock deep inside, and clamped his channel all around Jonah's hard length. "Fuck me now and make me come."

The second Christian's rectum squeezed down on Jonah's cock, it seemed a switch flipped inside Jonah. Jonah shouted hoarsely, straight-armed his palms into the floor on either side of Christian, and started to pound him in earnest. "Damn it, Sanchez"—he dropped his focus and looked between their bodies, shoving his hips into Christian vigorously with every hard pump—"wanted to be good for you."

"Too fucking good already." Christian dropped his legs, planted his feet into the mattress, and jammed his ass up to take every deep thrust. He let go of Jonah's butt and grabbed his own painfully hard erection, timing his rough yanking with every penetration of Jonah's cock. Christian winced but didn't slow down and didn't stop ramming his lower body up to meet every full shove of Jonah's fucking either.

With a half dozen more strokes in his ass and over his dick, Christian's balls contracted and pulled tightly against his body, too fast to grab hold of them and stave off the end. "Watch, watch." His gaze collided with Jonah's, Jonah's stare so damn intense it pushed Christian over the edge. "Ahh...shit..." Christian pulled hard on his shaft, his body jerking as release raced through him in a shivery rush. The first spray of ejaculate shot out of his slit and splashed on his chest. At the same time, his channel clutched Jonah, pulling him deep inside, hitting him with deep-seated pleasure on a whole different level. Christian ground his teeth together and pumped his dick for more as his body seized, coming again with another line of semen coating his torso.

Before the last spit fell from Christian's tip, Jonah's pupils flared, and he almost looked savage. He cried out and convulsed, and within seconds, Christian's walls stretched with the swelling of Jonah's prick. Wet heat filled Christian's ass as Jonah made a choking noise and succumbed to orgasm too.

No sooner did Jonah stop shaking than he grunted, dipped his head down, and started licking the cum from Christian's chest with big laps from his tongue. He swirled around Christian's nipples, sucking each one with powerful pulls. Without stopping for a breath, Jonah went the rest of the way up Christian's torso with equal thoroughness and intensity, and licked up the column of Christian's throat to under his chin, frantically over his jaw, until he found Christian's mouth and thrust his tongue inside. Jonah pulled at Christian's jaw, forcing it open with digging fingers, so hard Christian flinched and jerked his head back.

Rearing back, Jonah withdrew from Christian's ass in a flash and rose to his knees. "I'm sorry." Absolute horror shone clear in his eyes. "I lost it for a minute. I've never teased with anybody like that while fucking, and I didn't know where to stop. You came, and I love your cum, and I didn't think; I just started cleaning you like an animal, and once I started, your mouth wasn't that far away, and I like your mouth too, and I got carried away. Fuck, I probably left bruises all over you." He leaned in and fingered Christian's jaw, the touch so gentle it tore through Christian's already-obliterated heart. "I don't usually forget that I'm bigger than most people."

"Hey." Christian shot to his knees and clamped a hand over Jonah's mouth. "I can handle a few small bruises that come from what we just did." He smiled as he recalled the clamping hold he put on Jonah's bare ass. "It might surprise you tomorrow when you see a few on your body too." He took his hand away and smoothed it over Jonah's stubbly jaw. "As for the tongue bath"—he grinned again—"that's near the top of the fucking hottest things anyone has ever done to me."

Jonah cocked his head to the side. "Yeah?"

"Yeah." Christian nodded. Even as he said that, he couldn't deny the stickiness and sweat coating him. He shifted, grimacing at the tenderness in his backside he had known would occur. "However, after screwing twice, I'm gonna need a *real* bath as well." He rose to his feet, using the bed and Jonah's shoulder for leverage, and made his way to the hall.

That already-too-familiar heat didn't fire at his back, and Christian knew he stood alone. Pausing by the door, he looked back at Jonah and found the man still on his knees. "That was an invitation, you know." Christian's chest tugged as he realized he had to share the information out loud for the man to understand it. "Aren't you coming?"

"Do you really want me to?" Jonah's hands curled into fists against his thighs. His head almost dropped, but Christian caught Jonah stop himself and bring it back up before it fell. He even stood, and Christian swallowed hard at the picture of male beauty before him. "I've never taken a bath with anyone before."

Damn it. He kills me without even trying. Forgetting the nudity, Christian bit his cheek to keep from tearing up and forced a breezy smile to his face. "Well, since you're bigger and are going to take up most of the space, you'll be comfortable and like it just fine."

Jonah hesitated midstep. "We don't have to share. I can wait."

"You didn't let me finish." This time, Christian didn't try to hide anything. He looked Jonah up and down from top to bottom and openly appreciated every damn inch of perfection in front of him. When he had taken his fill—for the moment anyway—he strayed up and found Jonah's gaze in the shadows. "The upside of that for me is I have to sit on your lap."

A slow, sexy smile took over Jonah's face, transforming him. Damn, the man learned fast. "Oh. Okay. Right."

"Yeah. 'Oh, okay, right' is right. Hot water and a cramped space await." Christian crooked his finger and started walking slowly backward down the hall.

Jonah appeared quickly and moved in with the grace of a prowling cat, catching up in three smooth strides. "Fucking tease." Swooping down, Jonah planted his bulk into Christian's stomach and hoisted him over his shoulder. He spanked Christian on the ass and carried him through the house to the bathroom, threats of retaliation promised.

Christian laughed and smacked Jonah one right back. If what Jonah did tonight was his form of punishment, Christian couldn't wait to see what the man came up with next.

Chapter Nine

Christian slashed his roller across one of the dining room walls, giving the area a full second coating of paint. His gaze kept straying across the room to where Jonah painted the wall on the other side of the open hall, though, and his mouth watered at the man's wide shoulders encased in a white T-shirt and his amazing ass hugged by faded, paint-splattered jeans. God, Christian's palms had the shape and feel of Jonah's smooth, tight buttocks imprinted in their tactile memory, and they itched to pull Jonah's pants down and feel that firm flesh again. Shit, his lips and tongue tingled as well, just *thinking* about getting to taste Jonah one day, not just his ass or cock, but the rest of his body as well.

If Jonah ever gave him the opportunity.

Christian didn't know exactly what would happen next. He might have some trouble believing what happened last night was real, except for the fact that he had a tenderness in his rectum today that gave him ample proof it had. He had some light finger-mark bruising as evidence too; Jonah had been right about that. Christian had been equally correct, though; five small circle smudges of purple graced each of Jonah's ass cheeks where Christian had held him so tightly.

Christian got a good look at Jonah's backside when the man got out of bed to answer the door this morning.

More important than any of that, though, as proof of what they'd done, Christian had woken up in Jonah's arms this morning, and they'd shared a slow, unhurried kiss that had gone on until Rodrigo banged on the front door promptly at eight o'clock. Damn, Christian didn't think he'd ever had a more perfect moment in his adult life than lying on that mattress, the two of them on their sides, so fucking close they touched everywhere from knees, to stomachs, to lips, kissing and learning each other. And God, for Christian, the moment felt damn close to *loving* too.

As Christian stood in the dining room, painting all but forgotten, he swore he could feel Jonah's tongue slipping into his mouth and exploring, a taste as intense as Jonah's kisses of the night before, equally deep and needful, but somehow softer this morning. Jonah's complete focus on Christian when they kissed and fucked tickled renewed excitement in Christian's blood. As he thought about everything they did together last night, he stared at Jonah this morning and burned inside imagining that it—and more—might just happen again.

Jonah looked over his shoulder right then and caught Christian watching him red-handed. Jonah's pupils dilated, his nostrils flared, and he delivered Christian a look hot enough to break sweat out on the back of Christian's neck. Well, more sweat anyway. It was already shaping up to be another warmer-than-average March day. Christian chuckled at himself and the wildly erratic offshoots of his thoughts. Jonah smiled back, the gesture so clearly a natural reaction, from his gut, that Christian's breath stopped, trapped in his chest. *God, he's devastating when he smiles.*

Jonah turned back around and resumed painting, but Christian couldn't hold back his need to touch the bigger man. He walked across the room, moved in behind Jonah, and rubbed his palm across the small of Jonah's back. Jonah started, and Christian bit his lip to suppress another grin. He leaned up on the toes of his sneakers, looked around to make sure he acted discreetly, and pressed a quick kiss to Jonah's cheek. Warmth and the growth of stubble greeted Christian's lips, shooting a fast line of pleasure right into his belly and prick. Jonah nuzzled in, and Christian grazed his lips against Jonah's rough skin a second time, unable to help himself.

As Christian gave one last teasing lick, Jonah growled and turned. He captured Christian's mouth with his and turned the kiss into something purely carnal. Jonah pulled Christian against his front, holding him in a suffocating embrace as he plundered Christian's mouth with one of his voracious kisses. Christian opened up and kissed back just as roughly, accepting Jonah's thrusting tongue but then slowing him down with a hard suck, giving Jonah something Christian wanted to deliver to the man's cock. Wonderful *wanting* noises escaped Jonah and sank inside Christian, rushing a wash of pure pleasurable need through him in a shuddering wave.

"Fuck," Jonah uttered against Christian's mouth, his voice thick and low. "I love when I can feel you react like that." He swooped in on Christian again and slid his hand down Christian's back, cupping his ass. He pushed his fingers against Christian's crease, and Christian had never hated this pair of jeans more in his life.

"Oh good Christ." Rodrigo's voice cut through the house, tearing Christian and Jonah apart. Inhaling, trying to regain his breath, Christian found Rodrigo halfway deep in the living room, his hand gesturing up and down in their direction. "You're wasting perfectly good paint. If you're gonna stop to make out, at least put your rollers down so you don't end up painting each other's asses and backs."

Heat flamed through Christian, and Jonah's cheeks deepened in color too. They each still held a paint roller in hand, and Christian would bet they both had swipe marks of pale cream paint somewhere on their backs. At the same time, Christian couldn't keep the smile off his face, and Jonah had a light sparking in his eyes that outshone the blush, making Christian think he would not be averse to getting caught kissing again. *Damn.*

Abby *ahemed* and drew the men's attention to where she worked down the hallway toward the kitchen. "Don't listen to what he said." She crossed her arms under her breasts and lifted a brow past Christian and Jonah, right to Rodrigo on the other side. "You have no sense of spontaneity, Santiago. That was hands down the sexiest good morning, hello, or heck, just-because kiss I've ever seen in my life. If you couldn't see that, then you need to get out more and get yourself a personal life."

"Do you really want to start calling out each other's social lives, sweetheart?" A dangerously low tone laced Rodrigo's voice. He even took a step forward. "Because I feel very good putting mine up against yours any day of the week."

Abby made a defiant move forward too. "Bring it."

"Okay then." Christian spoke loudly, overriding the volume of the other two. He turned to Rodrigo and raised a brow. "Do you have news to share"—Rodrigo had stepped outside to make a phone call to one of his suppliers—"or did you just come back inside to bust my chops?"

Dark heat still burned in Rodrigo's eyes. He stared as if he looked right through Christian to Abby on the other side but finally clamped his jaw and put his focus on Christian. "We're good," he said. "They tracked the shipment, and the flooring will be delivered on Friday." Awareness softened the onyx chips hardening Rodrigo's gaze. "You want us to go ahead without you, or take the day off?"

"Wait a minute." Jonah grabbed Christian's arm and spun him around. "Why won't you be here on Friday?"

"Because—" *Oh wait, that's right, he doesn't know.* Christian had to stop for a moment and remind himself that Jonah actually knew very little about Christian's life. Vice versa too. "I'll be driving up to Tampa to visit my mom," Christian said. "She'll be expecting me."

Jonah's brow furrowed. He let go of Christian and took a step back. "You still have contact with your mom?" Jonah could not have looked more stunned if Christian had announced he would be a passenger on the next shuttle to the moon. "What about Marisol?" he asked. "You were so close to her. Shit, she left you in charge of taking care of her estate. You stayed with her for such a long time I figured the state must have granted her complete custody of you."

"They did, with my mother's full cooperation and consent." At Jonah's obvious confusion, Christian went ahead and shared further, even though he would have preferred privacy to talk about their personal histories. "Mari often took me to visit my mother while she was in prison, and my mother saw how well I was doing under Mari's care. My mother was young, and she wasn't educated, but that didn't make her ignorant or blind or stupid about her own situation or about me. Spending time in prison made her realize she really wasn't capable of taking care of me, not before she went in and not after she came out. She liked Mari, and Mari showed her respect in return. She wanted Mari to keep me after she was released, as long as Mari would let her stay in contact with me. Mari agreed. They worked out a formal agreement with the state, and for once, the system worked. Everyone did what was best for me. So yeah, I still know my mother. She has some problems, but I respect what she did for me, and Mari never let me forget that I should always show her respect for making a tough choice."

Jonah still looked like he had stepped off a bus onto an entirely new planet. "That's big of you. I don't know that I could be as forgiving."

"Different circumstances call for different outcomes." Unsure about Jonah, as the man had never spoken of his childhood, even for that short time under Mari's care, Christian chose his words carefully. "Maybe in your case, you shouldn't be."

"Different." Jonah's body went rigid, and his face seemed to turn to stone. "That's one word for it."

Jonah made Christian want to know all of his secrets and then hold him close and promise him everything would be okay. "Do you want to come with me?" Christian blurted, before he could think too deeply about rejection. "We could all take the day off from the renovations, and I could definitely use the company on the drive."

"Oh, uh..." Jonah shifted his weight from foot to foot. "I don't kn—"

"I could actually use the day off myself," Rodrigo cut in. "I need to check in on my other projects and look at rounding up orders for that work. We've been going really strong for a week, and I don't think it will hurt too much to step away for a day. I can come over in the morning, accept the delivery, and then lock up when I leave." Rodrigo looked past Christian and Jonah and pinpointed right in on Abby. "Do you have any problems with that?"

"Uhhhhh, no." Abby might as well have rolled her eyes. "Why would I?"

"Then good; we're settled. We'll all take care of other business on Friday." Rodrigo looked to Jonah. "Can you give me a hand?" He jerked his thumb toward the front door. "I want to double measure the porch and steps before I bring my equipment over and start sizing the wood."

"Yeah, sure. No problem." Jonah handed Christian his roller. "Hang on to that. I'll be right back."

Christian stared at Jonah as he walked outside, mesmerized by how smoothly Jonah moved for such a big man. There was nothing lumbering about him. Abby stepped in next to Christian and leaned her shoulder against his arm, watching as well. "Did you see how he just decided that for everyone?" she asked. "That man sure does like to throw his weight around."

Christian glanced at Abby, amused by her ire. She seemed to get her back up a hell of a lot with Rodrigo, just as Christian had done with Jonah not that long ago. "Rodrigo is his own boss and used to being in charge. He tends to be right, so I doubt he sees any point in changing."

Abby snorted. "I don't buy it. I'm my own boss too, and you didn't see me making a decision for everybody. Anyway"—she sidled in front of Christian and grabbed his arms—"enough about the almighty Mr. Santiago." Her blue eyes sparkled with excitement. "What about Jonah? Seriously, that was a hot kiss. And I saw that one in the parking lot through the rearview mirror, so I know it's not the first. What the heck is going on with the two of you?"

"I don't know." Abby and Rodrigo both knew Christian was gay. Beyond that, he didn't advertise himself or his feelings, but he also didn't lie. His gut already said Jonah wouldn't deny what had happened between them either. "We want each other, but we haven't really talked about it beyond that." Thinking about some of the other things Jonah had said last night, revealing such heartbreaking pieces of his soul, Christian couldn't fake *cool* about this surprising turn of events. "There's something about him, though, that always drew me to him, and it has only grown stronger since he came back. I want to know *this* man, who he is today, a thousand times more than the friendship I wanted with him when I was a kid."

"You mean the serious crush you had on him," Abby replied. "I may have been hiding in a corner most of the time

I was here with you guys, but I remember that night the cops took Jonah away. I remember you telling him that you loved him. That's a little more than wanting friendship."

"True enough." None of the other kids had ever harassed Christian about his outburst of emotion that night, but he knew they'd all witnessed it, and most of them understood what it meant. "I never did forget him. That was a crush, though, you are right. This…" His mind raced to find the right word. "This is different." At this point, Christian didn't know how to define what he and Jonah started last night. He wasn't sure Jonah did either. "I don't know what to say other than that."

"You don't have to say anything to me." Abby leaned in and gave him a quick hug. "Just be careful, not only with yourself, but with Jonah." Looking at him with such earnestness in her eyes, Abby rubbed his arms. "There's a lot of volatile stuff living right under the surface of that man, and I don't know how well he would handle finding out you're just living out a childhood crush after all."

Christian shook his head. "I would never do that to him. It's not—"

The phone rang, echoing through the house.

"Ooh, hold that thought." Abby jumped and raced toward the kitchen. "I bet that's the realtor," she said over her shoulder. Christian followed, keeping pace. "I've had two people slow down out front and ask me what's happening with this house. I went ahead and gave them her number. I know we're not on the market yet, but I wanted her to feel them out and see if they were serious."

Abby snatched the cordless phone off the cradle attached to the wall. "Hello?" There was a brief pause. "Sure. He's right here." She walked to where Christina stood at the entrance to the kitchen and handed the phone to him. "It's for you." As Christian put the paint rollers down, Abby added, "A Mr. Alan Mitchell."

Christian covered the mouthpiece and whispered, "That's Mari's attorney." He put the phone to his ear. "Hi, Mr. Mitchell. How are you this morning? Is everything all right?"

A long silence started tingling the hairs on the back of Christian's neck. Then, "I forgive you, Christian." David's familiar voice, not Mari's lawyer's, froze the blood in Christian's body. "You're grieving," he said, his voice eerily measured. "I know you still love me."

Christian clutched the back of his neck and looked up at the ceiling. "David, please stop. I don't. We're over."

"We're not." David's voice never changed pitch. "I know you still want to be with me as much as I want to be with you. I can wait for you."

Click. David hung up, and only a buzzing noise remained, vibrating loudly in Christian's ear. *Fuck. Fuck. Fuck.*

"Damn it." Jonah's voice sliced across the air and spun Christian around to where he stood in the dining room. Jonah's pale gaze homed in on Christian from ten feet away and chilled Christian in an entirely different way. Rodrigo stood right beside him. "That was him," Jonah said furiously. "It was that bastard David, wasn't it?"

Shit. Damn. And fuck again.

Clutching his hands into fists at his sides, Jonah's entire stance turned stony. "You don't have any color in your face right now, Christian, so don't even bother lying."

Christian went just as rigid as Jonah did. "I wouldn't lie to you, *Jonah.*" He strode to where Jonah stood, the cold leaving his body in a flash. "Yes. It was him, all right? It was David."

Granite didn't even begin to describe the hard set that took over Jonah's jaw. "Call the police and have him arrested," he ordered. "Do it. Right now."

Chapter Ten

Do it. Right now.

Jonah's order rang in Christian's ears just as loudly as David's obsessive whisper of a minute ago. Christian stood before the one he could deal with in this moment and silently counted to ten, then twenty, and then a few more before he felt he could even open his mouth, let alone speak without saying something he would regret. If they were going to become anything more than a two-time fuck, they needed to get a few things straight between them.

Right now.

Christian breathed out slowly, made eye contact with Jonah, and held himself in check for another good long moment before speaking. "Maybe you want to rephrase what you just said to me, and then we can have something more along the lines of a real conversation, rather than you issuing me an order."

Jonah leaned in on Christian, his clenched jaw ticking a mile a minute. "We already had that conversation when David showed up here unannounced," he whispered heatedly. "Now I'm telling you, this guy is fucking dangerous. If you don't want to do something about it to protect yourself, then I will."

His jaw dropping, Christian reared back. "What the hell do you mean by that?"

"What do you think I mean?" Jonah's face drained of color, but then he stiffened and sneered. "Look at you; I can tell you think you already know the answer. You think I'm gonna go beat the shit out of him. Or worse. I was locked up, right? So of course that's what I meant."

Christian reeled, barely able to keep up. "No, I don't think that. You think that." Jonah flinched, and Christian knew he had touched an exposed nerve. "That's what you see in yourself, so you assume everyone else thinks the same way. I just know that you can't take this over for me. This is my problem—"

"Of course," Jonah interrupted, "my bad." He threw his hands up. "I just thought the fact that we *fucked* last night made it my problem too. But you do whatever the hell you want. I guess I know where I stand now."

"Wow." Christian didn't know whether to throw a punch, laugh, or cry. "You just went from zero to one twenty in two seconds flat."

Jonah's fists dug into his outer thighs, and his entire being clenched tightly. His voice low and rougher than jagged rocks, he said, "I told you I don't know how to do this. I don't know what the hell I'm doing. Not even twenty-four hours in and I'm already screwing it up."

A band squeezed Christian's chest, erasing any indecision from his mind. This man made him want to cry, without a doubt. "Jonah, I'm not going to do a one-eighty on you and walk away just because something you say pisses me off."

Jonah jerked, looking as if someone took a swing at him. "Maybe you should." He turned, saw their audience, and bit off a curse, but came back to Christian and looked him squarely in the eyes once again. "The truth is I do want to go beat the crap out of David." He held his hand up before Christian even opened his mouth. "But I know better now than to do it. I won't." He forced those words out through clamped teeth. "No matter how much I want to."

"Yoo-hoo! Knock, knock!" Ida's familiar voice rang out from the front of the house, and everyone whirled in the direction of the door. Ida stood on the front porch, a huge pan in her hands. "May I come inside?"

Rodrigo stood the closest and rushed to let the woman in.

"Thank you, dear," Ida said. She stepped over the threshold, a big smile on her face. "Oh my goodness." She looked to the left and right and then turned, all while passing right by the group standing in the dining area, clearly on her way to the kitchen. "It hardly looks like the same house. So light and airy with these lovely clean walls. I still have paneling in my kitchen, but I might just speak to my nephew about taking a weekend and giving my kitchen new life. Yes, yes, he's coming for dinner tonight, and I just might do that."

Everyone followed Ida to the kitchen in one big pack. Christian put the phone down on the counter, and Ida set the pan down on the stovetop and peeled back the foil, releasing steam drenched with the scents of garlic, oregano, and tangy tomato sauce.

"I know you boys are working so hard over here," she said. She then quickly reached out and squeezed Abby's arm, her giant stone rings sparkling in the daylight shafting in through the window. "You too, sweetheart, so I thought I'd bring you something for lunch. This is my very own ziti recipe, already cooked. Enjoy, please."

"Thank you, Mrs. Santini," Christian said. "That's very generous of you." He stepped in and gave the woman a hug, but in truth hardly took note of the fantastic lunch or the murmurs of agreement from Abby, Rodrigo, and Jonah. Instead, Christian flipped back through the woman's kindly ramblings until he settled on the words that triggered his full attention. *My nephew.* Of course. Right.

"Mrs. Santini, how is your nephew doing?" Christian tried his damnedest to keep his voice casual. "I remember meeting him once or twice. Braden is his name, right? He's a cop?"

"He's a detective now," Ida answered. Her eyes lit up as she shared. "He passed the test and was promoted just six months ago. Do you remember when the janitor found that poor woman in the dumpster at the high school? Terrible stuff." She shivered. "That was Braden's first case as a detective, and they caught that man who did it, didn't they? Yes, they did. Braden is very smart, and he could see through that brother's lies right from the beginning." She brushed her fleshy palms against one another, as if she wiped away something foul. "That was a very bad man."

"Yes, he was." Christian nodded. He broached his topic with Ida carefully and chose his words even more so. "It has been a long time, and I would love to say hello to Braden again. If you think about it, would you mention that and ask him if he would pop over and say hi after having dinner with you tonight? I'd love to congratulate him on the promotion. He's also welcome take a look at the work we've done here and ask questions about removing paneling if he'd like."

Ida beamed, her rosy-lipped smile lighting up her entire face. "I will certainly do that. Now"—she moved to Christian and pecked a kiss on his cheek—"I must go." She touched the hands of the others before moving back down the hallway to the front door. "I still have three pans of ziti I have to deliver to the church, and I want to be home in time for my stories." Holding the screen door open, she paused and looked back at them, a youthful twinkle gleaming in her eyes. "They are getting very juicy. Bye now!" The screen door swished closed on that, and within a few seconds, she disappeared from sight.

Standing side by side, Christian stared at the vacated doorway. He could feel Jonah's presence right next to him and slipped his hand into Jonah's, holding it tight. "I'll talk to Braden and find out what my options are. I'll listen and consider everything he says. That's what I can promise. Okay?"

Christian held his breath, and after a moment, the rough pad of Jonah's thumb rubbed over the back of his hand, tingling Christian's entire arm to life.

"Okay," Jonah answered softly and squeezed Christian's fingers. "I can live with that."

Rodrigo moved in behind them and slung a muscled arm over each man's shoulders. "Good. You have harmony and a plan." He slapped a hard thump to Christian and Jonah's backs and then stepped away. "Now maybe we can get back to work. How does that sound?" He grabbed two rollers and thrust them at Christian and Jonah.

Abby threw something in about someone reminding Rodrigo that this wasn't one of his work sites, but Christian just shared a lingering, hot look with Jonah and got back to work.

* * *

"So that is what happened today," Christian said, finishing up sharing his information with Braden Crenshaw, who sat across from him at the kitchen table, "and I'm not sure where to go or what I want to do next."

Jonah paced the length of the kitchen, determined to keep his mouth shut. But fuck, he wanted to get right in this Braden's face and demand he tell Christian to file harassment charges against David as soon as possible. Jonah couldn't get much of a read on Braden, but the detective had a calmness in his pale green eyes that Jonah had a feeling could eventually break even the coldest of criminals. From the moment Jonah shook hands with Braden as Christian introduced them, Jonah sensed that Mrs. Santini's bragging about her nephew had not been familial pride at all, but the absolute truth of his capabilities. Now if he would just tell Christian to expose David for the obsessive, dangerous asshole he was, Jonah would believe Detective Crenshaw was as smart as the hype.

"You don't sound like you really believe David is dangerous," Braden said to Christian, drawing Jonah back into the conversation. "Be truthful with me here and take as long as you need to think about it before you answer. Is that denial, or do you genuinely believe it?"

Jonah held his breath, stopping to lean against the counter where he could see both Christian and Braden. Christian glanced his way. Jonah gave him a tight smile, wishing he knew how to fake things and offer Christian more comfort. He thought he should be doing something more to support Christian, but Jonah could not pretend he had mixed feelings about this David crap. He didn't. He had seen far too much in JD to take this kind of behavior lightly. He didn't for one second mistake that Christian's very life could be at stake.

After a long, dragged-out moment, Christian responded, "Like I said, we were friends in high school, and we got reacquainted when I moved home. We were in a sexual relationship for over a year, and I can honestly say there was never any violence in it."

"All right." Braden nodded. "How about manipulation? Did he try to make you feel guilty when you couldn't be with him or if he didn't get his way?"

"Maybe a little bit," Christian admitted. "But nothing that ever went on for a prolonged period, and I never sensed he was holding a grudge over to the next time we got together."

More nodding on Braden's part, and Jonah started chewing on the nubs of his nails.

"Would you describe David as passive-aggressive?" Braden asked.

Christian scrunched his brow and gave a little shrug. "Yeah, I suppose he could be that."

"What would you say his biggest fear is?"

"People finding out he's gay." Christian answered that without a pause. "We weren't ever more than passing friendly in public once I started telling the odd folk here and there that I was gay. In fact, I can't be sure, because I didn't know at first, but it wouldn't surprise me if that's when he started dating Carrie."

When Braden jotted down another fast note, Jonah almost pulled out his own hair. He swooped in, yanked out a chair at the table, and sat down. "What the hell does any of this shit matter?" Frustration turned Jonah's question into a fierce rumble. "The guy falsely identified himself as a lawyer so that he could get through to Christian on the phone. Consider how he must have thought about that before calling, because Abby said he readily identified himself as Mr. Mitchell without prompting. How did he know Marisol's attorney's name without either following Christian and seeing them together, or doing some research first? Either way, it's twisted, and it means he is becoming obsessive. I don't need to tell you where that leads and that a person like that can snap on a dime and turn violent."

Braden acknowledged Jonah with eye contact and then put his full attention right back on Christian. "The problem with bringing Mr. Joyner up on charges, as is the situation with a lot of these cases, is that there isn't a DA around who will touch this with a pair of rubber gloves. Yes, we have Ms. Gaines willing to say that a man identified himself as Mr. Mitchell, but after that, it's just your word against the other party as to who it was or what was said. We can confirm that Mr. Mitchell didn't make the call, but that doesn't automatically prove that Mr. Joyner did. You didn't record it, and the caller ID only brings up Unknown Name and Unknown Number. Do you know how likely it is that we would be able to get the phone company to trace that to an actual physical address we can link to Mr. Joyner?" Braden's face turned grim. "Not very, and that's just the truth. This isn't a procedural crime drama; it's real life."

Jonah slammed his fist against the table, rattling Braden's glass of water. "So then your answer is to sit back and do nothing, and wait for this bastard to get physical?" So much unchecked emotion—and fear—consumed Jonah that could hardly breathe. He shot up again, needing to move. "Unacceptable, Crenshaw." His chest rose, and his nostrils flared as he tried to regain control. "Unacceptable."

Jonah took three big strides, and when he reached the wall, he paused and took three deep breaths. Once he thought himself in better control, he turned...and found Christian right in his path. Dark eyes connected to Jonah and held him in their gaze, unwavering, and Jonah swore this man was a thousand times tougher and stronger than he could ever hope to be. Jonah's chest squeezed, and his throat hurt. He cupped his hand around Christian's neck and leaned down until their foreheads touched. Fuck, he didn't have the needed words.

Christian didn't seem to require them. He wrapped his hand around Jonah's forearm and held on. "It's okay, Jonah." He brushed a soft kiss high on Jonah's cheekbone. "It's going to be all right."

"No, it's not okay," Braden said from the table, pulling Christian and Jonah apart and back to him. They each took a seat again. "So here's what I'm going to do, and what you're going to do. You're going to get a journal, and you're going to write down every time David contacted you after you told him to leave you alone. Make note that you're doing this after it happened so that nobody thinks you're trying to deceive them. From now on, any time David makes contact with you again, in person, by phone, or text, through e-mails, you make a note in that journal. If you can record your phone conversations, all the better. If there's a text you can save, that's excellent evidence. If he confronts you in person, if there is someone with you, have them make a note of it too, as a witness. Even better, if you have a cell phone that can take a picture, snap one of him right in front of you, and that will have a time and date stamp on it. In addition to that, make a note of what was said in the conversation in your journal as well."

Braden paused and made a quick note on his sheet of paper. "Now here's what I'm going to do. First, I'm going to talk to someone and see if a restraining order can be issued, at the very least. I'm not sure you have enough right now, quite honestly, so don't get your hopes up too high about that. I really don't think you have enough for a harassment case." He shifted in his seat, and the light over the table caught the strands of silver weaved into the dark hair at his temples. "At least not one that is going to go anywhere. You have to decide if pressing criminal charges is something you're ready to do. Once you make that step, you can't take it back. If you change your mind, you can't just drop the charges. You can choose to no longer cooperate, but at that point, it would be in the hands of law enforcement and the DA to decide how they want to proceed."

"But the damage will be done publicly," Christian said, "as far as David will be concerned. People will know he was in a relationship with me, and whether it should or not, it will destroy him." Christian paled, and his eyes looked bleak. "I'm not interested in destroying David. I don't want to expose his secrets or wreck his wife's life when she finds out, as well as putting a big jolt through his family. That's not who I am. I just want David to leave me alone. That's all."

"I understand where you're coming from, Chris," Braden answered. He folded the piece of paper Christian had provided him and slipped it into his pocket. "Give me a day or two to quietly look into that restraining order and see if there's even a possibility it can happen. In the meantime"— he stood and, in doing so, brought Jonah and Christian to their feet too—"I'm going to have an off-the-record talk with David." He held up his hand. "Don't worry; I won't do it at his home or at work, nothing to call attention to him by anyone who knows him. I want to feel him out myself, just to see if I sense something that needs immediate attention. I'll have a friendly conversation with him and let him understand you're serious and are one step away from officially getting the police and lawyers involved in what he's doing. I'll very rationally lay out that he might want to think about the consequences of that in deciding if he really wants to continue to put himself in your life—in any way— ever again." The edge of Braden's lip moved, but Jonah couldn't say it was exactly a smile. Braden stuck his hand out Christian's way. "Sometimes all it takes is one gesture to make a person realize there will be consequences to their choices. A detective having a chat with him might do it. Sound good?"

"Yes, thank you." Christian clasped Braden's outstretched hand and shook it. "Very much. I know you thought you were only coming over here to say hi and look at walls. I appreciate your patience and sharing your expertise."

"No problem." Braden nodded at Christian, then shifted and shared a firm handshake with Jonah too. That done, he started down the hallway toward the front door. "The house really does look great. Aunt Ida was telling me about Mrs. Ramirez's wishes for it over dinner, and I'm sure you're going to get a nice price for it." Braden had already expressed his sympathy shortly after saying hello.

"Thank you. We hope so," Christian answered. He pushed the front door open and held it for Braden. Christian followed Braden to the porch, and Jonah followed Christian, unwilling to leave his side.

Already down the steps, Braden lifted his hand as he crossed the lawn to his aunt's drive. "I'll be in touch."

Jonah and Christian stayed on the porch, watching in silence until Braden's car was no longer in sight.

Christian didn't make a move to go back inside; he just shoved his hands in his pockets and kept staring toward the end of the street. "Think it will work?" he eventually asked, his words a hush.

Christ. Christ. Christ. Once again, Jonah wished he could invent an answer that would make Christian feel better. Instead, he murmured, "Don't know."

Pulling his hands out of his pockets, Christian scrubbed his face. "God, I'm so tired." The porch light cast Christian's face in unusual shadows, drawing Jonah's attention to the smudges under Christian's eyes. "Of all of it."

Jonah's heart lurched, hurting him in a way it never had before. "I know." He pulled Christian against his chest and held him close. Damn it, Jonah didn't know exactly what Christian needed, he just knew *he* needed to hold Christian right now and couldn't fight it. He brushed a kiss against the top of Christian's head and even found himself rocking them a little bit. "I know."

Jonah felt maybe he had done the right thing when Christian wound his arms around Jonah's back and burrowed in close, as if he never wanted to let go.

That was okay with Jonah. He would stand on this porch holding this man all night, and more.

Whatever Christian needed.

Chapter Eleven

Fingers danced lightly along Jonah's arm, bringing forth a shiver. Eyes still closed, he enjoyed the last remnants of half sleep. He nuzzled his cheek into the pillow, settled his front more comfortably into the mattress beneath him, and smiled at the unique blanket keeping his back warm.

Christian lay on top of Jonah, covering him, teasing Jonah's skin from his forearm up to his shoulder and back with soft touches. Contentedness settled on Jonah, and he thought maybe, just maybe, he wasn't a complete idiot and could figure this relationship stuff out after all. He knew one thing for sure; he liked Christian draped on his back, and every gut instinct that had kept him out of trouble in juvenile detention, as well as after his release, told him that this—this very moment—was *right* and *safe.*

This was a relationship.

And Jonah was knee-deep in it. With a naked man on top of him.

Jonah smiled into his pillow, unable to hold it back.

"So you are awake," Christian murmured at his ear. "I thought I could feel a change in the tension in your body, but I wasn't sure."

If Christian would only slide his hand under Jonah to take a feel of his cock, he would realize a definite change in Jonah's body had occurred just a few minutes ago. Maybe another time. Jonah hadn't given Christian a chance to be anything more than the full recipient of his need for sexual contact, and he was a little bit afraid to ask Christian to turn the tables. Jonah groaned inwardly. Christ, he didn't want to be anywhere else than in Christian's capable control. Jonah's morning erection swelled between his stomach and the mattress just thinking about Christian consuming him, as if his member reached for Christian's touch.

Christian's fingertips drew a line over Jonah's shoulder, tickling him into a chuckle.

Jonah would have tried to lean back and deliver a glare, but he didn't want to move and risk Christian crawling off him. "What are you doing?" he asked instead, biting his cheek to stifle another ridiculous shiver.

"Right now, I'm tracing the lines of your tattoo." Christian moved his fingertips again, and now that he knew what Christian did, Jonah could sense Christian's finger mapping the outer shape of the tattooed wing. "It's really beautiful; I love the way it reaches over your shoulder and also dips down your upper arm and back. It makes me sad too, for some reason." Christian paused and brushed his lips against Jonah's shoulder. "I don't know why."

Nervousness started buzzing through Jonah, as it always did when he thought about the terrifying times right after being released from JD. "Where are you from, Christian?" His heart rate increasing, Jonah scrambled for a different subject. "Every once in a while, I can hear a slight accent with certain words. I remember it being a little more pronounced when you were younger."

"I'm from here; I was born in Florida," Christian answered. He had his cheek against the back of Jonah's neck and, between his fingers still playing with Jonah's skin and his warm breath fanning that same flesh as he spoke, Jonah could barely focus on Christian's words. "My mom was from Venezuela, though, and she didn't come to America until she was sixteen. She still has a difficult time with English. When I was little, my mom and I spoke only Spanish at home. It's the same when I go to visit with her now. I spoke English at school, and when we went out to stores, I usually talked to the clerk and translated for my mom. That's probably why a hint of an accent still comes out occasionally when I talk, because of her."

Jonah sometimes felt like he functioned within a population that knew a secret language he didn't, so at least in that one regard, he could sympathize with Christian's mother's plight. "That must be tough for her. It probably feels very isolating, and I would guess becomes more so as she gets older."

"She has found little tricks here and there to help compensate." Christian shifted his legs off the lines of Jonah's and tucked himself in between Jonah's thighs. Christ, it felt good. "Plus, there are a lot more retailers with Spanish-speaking staff available these days. A lot has changed since I was with her as a kid."

"I suppose."

"You don't want me asking about your tattoos, do you?" Christian cut right through Jonah's quick-change tactic. "If you don't want to talk about them, it's okay with me." He slid his hands down Jonah's arms and threaded his fingers between the backs of Jonah's, locking them together in yet another way. "You didn't have to change the subject."

Silently, in absolute stillness, Jonah breathed through the ridiculous wave of panic that swamped him where he lay. *It's not a state secret, Roberts. It's not a secret, period. It's okay to share with someone. With Christian.* "I had that one done right after I got out of JD." His face and body grew heated with every word, making him grateful for the morning shadows. "I felt kind of free, like a bird, so I had a guy ink a wing on me. It's a bird's wing, not an angel."

Christian shifted again, and fuck, blood raced painfully to Jonah's cock as the man's dick rubbed against Jonah's taint and balls. Christian went right on, as if he couldn't feel *exactly* what the hell his body was doing to Jonah. "It's a pretty big tattoo," Christian said. "Could you only afford to do one side?"

The cold splash of his younger life almost killed Jonah's slow burn to arousal hell. "That's not why." Humiliation tore through Jonah, and he fought an internal battle to protect himself, to cover a shame that lived embedded in every fiber of his being. "Deeper down, I didn't feel like I could fly like a real bird, so I only got the one wing."

"Jesus, man." Christian shuddered against Jonah's back. "Sometimes you say things that break my heart."

Any embarrassment would be better than this exposure—even rejection. "Right now, I'd kill if you would take care of an entirely different organ for me." He pushed his half erection into the mattress, giving it some friction.

"Fuck it, Christian. I want to feel your mouth on my cock more than just about anything."

Christian strong-armed up from Jonah's back, crushing Jonah's hands.

"Oow." Jonah curled his hands into fists and, in the process, tilted Christian off him to the side. "I'll need those hands again."

"Sorry." Sliding off Jonah completely, Christian lined himself right up against Jonah's side, putting their faces only inches apart. "Can I really touch you?" His gaze somehow found Jonah in the semidarkness and pinned him in place. "Or are you just trying to change the subject again?"

Jonah should have known this direct, forthcoming Christian still existed beneath the surface of the more introverted man he'd met again a week ago. Jonah had witnessed and been the focus of *this* Christian time and again during his original stint in Marisol's home. "How about both?" he confessed reluctantly. "If I admit to that, will it get me what I want?"

Christian lifted his hand and brushed the back of it against Jonah's temple. "Asking will get you what you want, Jonah. You don't ever have to do anything else." Christian's eyes shone bright with all kind of impossible promises, ones that, when looking at Christian, caused Jonah to slip into the dangerous place of a believer.

"I want you to do everything with me, Christian." Jonah's throat squeezed, making his confession thick and tight. "Everything I've done to you, I want the same and more. Whatever you want, I want too."

Moving his hand from Jonah's temple to the back of his neck, Christian pulled Jonah in until their faces touched. "That's about the sexiest thing anybody has ever said to me." He pressed his lips to Jonah's with a grin. "And about the sweetest too." Just as innocently as Christian smiled, he licked across Jonah's lips, probing until he broke through the seam and took a taste that fired all through Jonah's tightly strung body. Barely giving Jonah time to kiss him back, Christian retreated and pressed another chaste kiss on Jonah's mouth. "Now roll on your back and let me take care of your cock."

Jonah complied, his desire for this moment far stronger than any latent embarrassment or fears. Once on his back, he stretched, his thighs straightening and then relaxing, his body undulating, and his erection jutting, pointing toward his belly. He reached down and stroked himself, so used to taking care of his own arousal that his arm moved before he it gave a conscious command.

Looking his fill, Christian rumbled an appreciative noise and crawled on top of Jonah again, knocking his hand away. He settled in, much in the way he'd been on Jonah's back two ticks ago. "Damn it, Jonah." He rubbed their cocks, stomachs, and chests together. "You have the most insane body."

"And you're making it feel very out of control." Nearly crying out with the pleasure of Christian's moves, Jonah squirmed and rolled his hips as every nerve ending inside him reached and strained for more contact with Christian. "Jesus, man." Jonah inhaled sharply through clenched teeth as their dicks grazed again. "I think I'm gonna come."

Christian slid down a bit but looked up with those mesmerizing brown eyes of his. "Not yet, baby." He pressed a light, tongue-dipping kiss to the center of Jonah's torso and then another one just a hair below it. "Let me get there first." With another brush of his lips and tiny flick of his tongue, Christian methodically worked a slow line down the center of Jonah's front, evoking tremble after tremble in Jonah.

Every kiss on Jonah's stomach felt like a lick to his cock, and he started pumping his hips into Christian's abdomen in time with each tantalizing touch. He leaked like a broken faucet, smearing early cum into Christian's hard flesh on every small thrust, releasing evidence of just what Christian's seduction did to him. Jonah lifted to his elbows, watching through a slitted gaze as Christian's dark head inched ever closer to his goal. Christian paused and dipped his tongue into Jonah's navel, and Jonah got so damn excited his entire body jerked, jolted by the small intimacy. He swore to God he felt Christian smile at the reaction, his lips turning up against the flat of Jonah's belly.

Reaching Jonah's second tattoo, Christian lapped all around the light and dark wings surrounding a key, licking almost like a dog, all the while avoiding Jonah's cock, straining right in front of him, crying for that first contact. Christian kissed the center of the tattoo and once again looked up, finding Jonah's eyes. "You'll tell me about this tattoo too." Christian finally, finally, wrapped his hand around Jonah's erection and brought the tip to his lips. "One day." He then went right down on Jonah's cock, taking him to the throat on the first long suck.

Jonah hissed long and low, his muscles stiffening and locking up tight as Christian surrounded his length and delivered wet, suctioning heat from tip to root. He did it again, and the top of Jonah's head nearly blew clean off. Jonah had been given blowjobs by men and women before, but never by someone he ached for, well beyond the sex. This was *Christian's* head bobbing up and down, *Christian's* tongue licking him, *Christian's* mouth sucking on him. Shit, even *Christian's* teeth occasionally grazing him, and it all had Jonah moaning, his hips going crazy with every slight or big move.

Staring, captivated, and panting, Jonah watched Christian go down, stuffing Jonah's cock deep into his mouth. He didn't stop until Jonah's thick head kissed Christian's throat, and only then pulled off and revealed Jonah's saliva-covered prick, one inch at a time. The wide O of Christian's open lips, his lust-dark eyes, the way he held Jonah's thighs apart, the murmuring noises he made—which vibrated all the way through Jonah's stiff dick—all painted a carnal 3-D picture Jonah had very little strength to combat.

Just when Jonah didn't think he could take any more, Christian licked a line down the underside of Jonah's cock, kept right on going, and slurped Jonah's nuts into his wonderful mouth. He sucked and pulled on Jonah's sac with an exquisite agony that Jonah never wanted to end. Unable to command his hand to stop, Jonah reached down and grabbed his erection, jerking himself off in an overhanded rough pull, his body writhing so wildly he had no idea if he wanted to hold back or rush to release. Even if he wished for the former, in this moment, he had no ability to control or direct his body's needs.

Without letting up on tonguing Jonah's balls, Christian released Jonah's right thigh and joined Jonah's hand on his penis, covering it and adding greater tightness and force to every drag on Jonah's painfully hard length. Every molecule in Jonah's cock sat right at the surface, just under his skin, shrieking to let loose the explosion coiling within.

Jonah spread his legs even farther apart and dug his feet into the floor on either side of the narrow mattress, looking for traction that might hold him to this earth for just a moment longer. His body glistened with sweat, his legs and arms shook with tension, and his spine tingled with pure joy. Jonah knew he couldn't take another damn thing, and then Christian pushed his fingers between Jonah's cheeks and tickled his pucker, shoving Jonah right into the abyss.

His dick swelling, his ass clenching, and his balls tightening within the confines of Christian's mouth, Jonah uttered gutturally, "Ohhh, damn it, damn it... I'm coming..." Just as Jonah lost it, Christian released his testicles and jumped back up to Jonah's cock, wrapping his lips tightly around the head. Orgasm raced through Jonah's length in a fiery shot. He came hard in Christian's mouth, shouting as the sensation, so purely raw and sexual, jerked him, making him spurt again. Jonah groaned endlessly as it happened, and his upper body twisted in the throes of orgasm, contorting as he fought his way through an entirely new level of release.

Feeling as if he were coming unglued but unable to stop it, half on his side now, Jonah frantically reached for Christian and pushed his face out of his crotch. "Fuck me, Christian. Take me. I need it right now."

Christian's eyes darkened to beyond the color of a moonless night. He scrambled onto his knees. "Fuck, you turn me on. Damn it." He hauled Jonah's ass and hips up onto his thighs. "Give me the lube."

Quickly, before Jonah could process Christian's words, Christian shifted Jonah's left leg, laying it straight against Christian's chest, exposing Jonah's crease and putting his bud within touching distance of Christian's cock. Christian drenched two fingers in his own spit and pushed up through Jonah's crack, stopping only when he reached Jonah's asshole. Pressure tapped against Jonah's sphincter, making his hole tighten and his channel contract. *Fuck.* Christian probed his fingers against Jonah's pucker again, and Jonah's dick started to harden on anticipation alone. He couldn't breathe properly or make his heart rate slow down, and if he had to wait a second longer, he wasn't sure he would survive to feel the first slide of Christian's dick in his ass. He could live with a little bit of pain, but Christian preparing him for a gentler ride might just do Jonah in.

The tips of Christian's two fingers pushed at Jonah's entrance again. Pressing against the powerful little muscle with insistence, Jonah felt certain one more stab would breach his bud and take his ass.

Suddenly frantic, Jonah knocked Christian's fingers away, snapping Christian's downturned gaze up to his. "Your cock." Jonah threw his arm above his head and grabbed the lube off the bookshelf, knowing right where he put it late last night. He popped the lid open and strained his body up just enough, upending the stuff over Christian's dark, rearing erection. He squeezed some out and tossed the tube aside, only taking time to circle his hand around Christian's cock, rubbing in the cool substance. "I want your cock inside me first," he said, his voice unduly harsh.

Their complete focus remained riveted to each other, their faces and bodies striped with shadows and light through the pattern created by the window blinds. Jonah shifted his own hips and pulled Christian's dick to his quivering hole. "Fuck me, Christian." His entire body shook for it. "Now."

An inhuman sound rumbled through Christian, matching the glint of feral wildness sparking in his eyes. Christian took bruising hold of Jonah's legs, jammed forward, and speared his cock home in one sure thrust, collapsing Jonah's hole and invading his channel on the other side.

Jonah cried out with the sheer pleasure and pain of it as his ass clamped down in a spasm all around Christian's dick. Christian jerked and shoved deeper, taking more of Jonah's tight channel and driving Jonah's shivering anus into a frenzy.

Christian wrapped his arms around Jonah's leg against his chest, holding him close, and started a furious pounding in Jonah's rectum, setting Jonah's chute on fire. Christian wore an almost-pained expression as he fucked Jonah with deep, fast strokes, and it was the most stunning picture of beauty Jonah had ever witnessed. Jonah couldn't look away, and it seemed that Christian couldn't either. Each hard strike of Christian's cock into Jonah's ass became a twin moment of connection between the men, where the physical taking swirled and mingled with stripped emotions that could not be hidden in such a naked display.

Jonah worked himself off on Christian's buried erection, gasping as the first shock of discomfort left his body and strains of pure physical pleasure jolted through him, sizzling through his channel and cock right up his spine. He gritted his teeth and ground down on Christian's taking of him, reaching for more, greedy for every inch Christian could give him, until Christian consumed him in every way and he could stand to feel no more.

Struggling with his need, Jonah straightened his arms and lifted his upper body, planting his hands into the sheet covering the mattress to help hold him in place. Christian sawed down on Jonah's body, hitting his chute at a different angle, and unfathomable desire raced through the entirety of Jonah's being, all the way into the very tips of his fingers and toes.

Jonah moved his left foot off the floor, planted it against Christian's shoulder for leverage, and bounced his ass over Christian's embedded length in a frantic flurry. "Oh, fuck, Christian." Jonah could see little more than a lust-induced blur of Christian, as his rectal walls rippled around Christian's dick in a wonderful wave. "So good...feels so damn good."

Christian jerked and cursed. He yanked Jonah's calf to his mouth and bit, stinging Jonah's flesh with sweet pain. "You're the only one." The words slipped out of Christian, almost unrecognizable beneath the roughness and sharp intakes of breath. The fog cleared, and Jonah saw right into Christian's eyes, clear as with full daylight. "I've never fucked anyone but you."

Jonah's chest seized. "You…" His body became one giant pulsing heartbeat, stealing his words. Release, need, connection took Jonah over, and in a split second, he stilled and then started jetting hot streams of seed across his stomach and chest as he came. His ass clenched all around Christian's cock at the same time, holding him tight inside, and Christian needed no more than that to give up his fight. He gripped Jonah's hips and kept their bodies snugly connected, hissing long and steady, orgasm overtaking him. Christian warmed Jonah from the inside out, releasing a shitload of cum deep inside Jonah's ass. Jonah shuddered through the intimacy of it, and Christian trembled too.

As the last ebb of orgasm left Jonah's body, his legs went lax and fell to the sides of Christian's thighs, his strength gone. In the same heartbeat, Christian exhaled and fell forward onto Jonah's chest, his cock slipping free of Jonah's ass as he let all his weight press right into Jonah's torso. Jonah zinged inside, thrilling at the feel of a sated Christian lying on top of him. If he could figure out how to make it work, Jonah would take a scenario like this every night of the week.

Long minutes passed in silence, the only thing of note in the room the steady, *together* rise and fall of chests and abdomens as Jonah and Christian's breathing slowly returned to normal.

Eventually, Christian wiggled against Jonah, smearing ejaculate over their stomachs. He nipped Jonah's chin and then his mouth, and finally found his eyes. "That was insane." A little smile lilted Christian's lips up, but his gaze quickly sobered. "How about you? Are you okay?"

Every inch of Jonah's body buzzed, on the inside and out, and he didn't think he had understood what trusting someone meant until the moment Christian penetrated his body. He smiled, hoping he didn't look like a complete idiot, but at the same time unable to stop. "Hell yeah." His face heated, but he couldn't stop. "You can do that to me again, anytime."

"Oh, well…" Christian dipped down and sank into a kiss, his tongue slipping inside for a slow tangle of wet heat. He withdrew his tongue and flicked the tip against Jonah's nose. "Good morning then."

"To you too."

The doorbell rang loudly through the house.

Rodrigo.

Damn.

Christian broke the kiss and dropped his forehead to the pillow. "Son of a bitch." Jonah thought he might have heard Christian growl. "I'm really beginning to hate having my own personal human alarm clock."

A chuckle rumbled through Jonah, and he talked down the hard-on trying its best to emerge for the third time. "We need to get that guy laid."

Hoisting up to his knees, Christian reached for a pair of jeans. "You ain't kidding." He used the edge of the sheet to wipe drying cum from his belly and then threw on a T-shirt. "I'll get it." He pushed to his feet and made his way to the door. "This time you can use the shower first."

Jonah fumbled and found a pair of jeans too. "Thanks. I won't be long."

Christian paused, his hand wrapped around the doorjamb. The doorbell gonged again, but he didn't move. He looked at Jonah and stood there for a good long moment in silence, staring, before he finally said, "Thanks for agreeing to drive with me to Tampa today." Christian's words came out a little scratchy, scraping at Jonah's heart. "It means a lot." Christian disappeared down the hall before Jonah could say a word.

* * *

Silence reigned between Jonah and Christian on the ride home from Tampa. The truck drove smoothly on the less-traveled state roads, the landscape becoming more and more familiar to Jonah, no matter the time that had passed him by. The trip up from Coleman had been nice, with Christian sharing a bit more about his childhood, his mother, and the constantly evolving state of their relationship. Jonah felt gutted by Christian's trust and openness; he was equally twisted up inside when for every story or moment Christian shared, Jonah gave him nothing in return.

The age-old oak trees that blurred by on either side of the truck as they drove called to Jonah, reminding him that memories of his own childhood lived still, not that far away.

"Take a left here," Jonah said abruptly, pushing the words out before they choked him. "I want to show you something."

Christian shot him a quick, curious look but put his focus right back on the road and did as told. Jonah didn't give any explanation, only directions on where to turn when needed. Getting closer to their destination, and the very fact that Christian followed without question, broke sweat out on Jonah's neck and made his T-shirt cling to his back. Christ, this was stupid. Jonah didn't want to do this.

Tucked away in rural country, the interstate and closest town behind them, a dirt road loomed, overrun with too-tall grass on either side. Jonah would have to do something about that soon.

"Turn here." Jonah pointed, unable to say more.

Christian complied, not stopping until the dirt path came to an end. When he could go no farther he cut the engine, left the keys jangling in the ignition, and turned to Jonah. "What is this?" he asked, his voice hushed.

Nothing but grass loomed ahead now, but as Jonah stared through the windshield, he could see three run-down trailers in his mind, clear as day.

"This"—he quaked where he sat—"is hell."

Chapter Twelve

Christian sat facing Jonah in the truck but didn't know what to say.

This is hell. The echo of Jonah's words sent another chill down Christian's spine.

How did one respond to such a statement?

Christian reached out and touched Jonah's forearm, and the man jumped. "Sorry," Christian murmured and withdrew his hand to his side of the seat.

Jonah shook his head, sparing Christian a sidelong glance. "It's okay." His focus went right back to the field of overgrown grass ahead. A moment later, he rubbed his palms on his jeans. "It's not you. It's *this.*" Even in profile, his face looked stark and faraway. "It's where I lived until I was fourteen years old."

Shit. Tentatively, Christian approached again, but only verbally this time. "Do you want to get out of the truck and take a look, or would you rather just stay here?"

"We can get out." Jonah didn't wait for Christian before opening his door and sliding out himself. "I'm fine."

Christian wasn't so sure about that, but he climbed out anyway and followed Jonah to the front of the truck. The sun and humidity beat down on them in crushing waves, but Christian looked to Jonah and saw goose bumps marring his arms. Everything in Christian's nature said to offer comfort, but something in Jonah's stance told him to hang back and let Jonah do this on his own terms.

Jonah exhaled a shaky breath and, while staring ahead, just started talking. "There used to be three trailers on this land. There"—he pointed to the left—"there"—straight ahead—"and there." He made a final wave with his hand to the right. "First one was where we lived, unless my mom was *working*"—Jonah's mouth twisted—"trying to earn some money to support her habit. I had to go outside when the men came." Jonah turned suddenly, laying a too-bright stare on Christian. "You know how to make meth?"

Shaking his head, Christian fought down the pressure that built behind his eyes. Jonah did not need to see tears. "No, I don't."

"I do." Jonah's body tightened, and his face turned harder than stone. "My dad taught me how in the trailer that was there." He turned away again, nodding his head to his right as he did. "Well, I thought he was my dad anyway. We lived here with him. Charlie—that was his name. He was my mom's source, but he wasn't giving stuff to her for free. Anyway, I thought Charlie was my dad; I called him that, and he never said I shouldn't. I don't remember any other man in my childhood, and I have no memory of living anywhere but on this land with Charlie and my mom before I went into the system. Turns out Charlie wasn't my father after all. After my mom died, Charlie kept me for a short while, up to when he met a new woman with a kid of her own. He turned me over to the state then, saying I wasn't his legal or biological responsibility. I found out then his name wasn't listed as the father on my birth certificate; nobody's was. A DNA test confirmed it, so he didn't have any trouble washing his hands of me."

"I'm sorry." Christian's eyes fell closed on the wave of pain Jonah radiated, probably completely unaware that those around him could feel it, all the time. For Christian, it hit him in the gut, right now, stronger than ever. Unable to stop himself, no matter if it was right, Christian moved in and wrapped his arms around Jonah from behind, holding tight to his waist. He rested his cheek against the man's shoulder blade and spoke roughly into his shirt. "I'm so, so sorry."

Jonah shrugged, but it felt unsteady against Christian's front. "It didn't seem to matter to Charlie that I thought he was my father for the first fourteen years of my life, and that he never gave any hint that he wasn't. Not that he was nice or anything; there were times when he was downright cruel to my mom and me. The scar I have on my eyebrow is from when he shoved me across the trailer and my forehead hit the corner of the table."

Holy shit. The matter-of-fact way Jonah talked cut Christian up inside, making him grieve in place of a man who clearly wouldn't.

"He wasn't always like that, though. My mom and I had our uses, so I guess that's why he let me call him Dad and kept us around. When he was away, or *busy* with my mom, someone had to be here to answer the door and sell the drugs. That was me."

Tension locked Jonah rigid as steel, but his voice remained distant and calm. "Charlie also sold pot. That's what was in the middle trailer. He grew marijuana in there. I knew how to tend that too." Finally a crack in the stance; Jonah covered Christian's hands on his stomach and clamped on tight. "Some scary-ass people came to this place to get their next fix, some of them with nasty teeth and gaunt bodies that made them look like skeletons. Gave me a hell of a lot of nightmares about zombies and about what they might do to me if I didn't have the drugs to give them or a gun to protect myself.

"At the same time, you have no idea how many people who look like upstanding citizens knocked on our door and thought it was cute that a little kid was making drug transactions. Men in expensive suits and women who looked like moms shopping in the grocery store. College kids, teenagers, you name it; they all dealt with me and never once commented that it was wrong or reported it to the authorities, even anonymously. Shit." Jonah's voice cracked. "I was homeschooled, and I hardly ever had contact with people who weren't buying or selling, but even I figured out enough through watching TV that I shouldn't be doing what Charlie was making me do. At least *one fucking person* should have thought it was wrong enough to tell someone before it was too late."

"They should have." Christian nodded, transferring the agreement against Jonah's back. "You're absolutely right. Someone should have stood up and protected you."

"Yeah." Jonah breathed deeply, the act rising and falling Christian behind him. Christian wasn't sure the breath was a cleansing one yet, but it seemed Jonah had an easier time taking the second one, and even a bit more so with the third. "Yeah."

Christian's blood heated as he thought about Jonah's childhood. He wasn't prone to violence, but after playing minor league ball for six years, he knew how to throw a punch—or three. He would love to put his fist in that fucker Charlie's face right this second. Someone needed to do it, for Jonah. The injustice of it all burned through Christian, and he had a hell of a hard time keeping the edge out of his voice. "How did Charlie get away with handing you over to the state without bringing a heap of shit down on himself?"

A cynical laugh shook Jonah, taking Christian right back to a place of cold. "Trailers are mobile, Christian. Do you think anything more than one innocent single-wide sat on this property when my mom died, or when DCF came and collected me? Do you think either one of us had a hint of the smell from the meth chemicals remaining on our skin or clothes when Charlie turned me in? No, he hosed me and scrubbed me down good, and he temporarily moved the drug trailers and had someone else tend to them for a good week before he reported me and gave me away. Charlie looked like a wuss, not like the smart bastard he was. Nobody suspected for one second—or maybe they didn't care enough to ask— that he controlled the drugs that caused my mom to die. He just looked like a sucker that had been pussy-whipped. People don't dig or ask questions when someone isn't right there on their shoulder demanding it. The resources don't exist. The truth is most people are so jaded they're perfectly willing to believe that a pretty girl who hooked on the side and had a bad habit could seduce a sad-sack john into thinking her kid was his, and that he didn't learn the truth until after her tragic death. People don't want to see more. They don't have the time."

Christian wished he could disagree, but knowing that too many kids didn't make it to the safety of a home like Marisol's kept him silent.

Seconds slowly ticked into minutes. Christian kept holding Jonah, letting him take his time looking into the open space that he surely saw as it had existed all those years ago. Christian concentrated on Jonah's breathing, which, while still a little fast, seemed more under control.

Abruptly, Jonah said, "I own this land now," shocking the shit right out of Christian. "I looked the deed up right after I got out of JD, just to see if Charlie still owned it. He did. For some reason that picked at me, even though I couldn't do anything about it. I kept watching it though, checked it every so often online, and then eventually had a local realtor keep her eye on it. I guess Charlie hurt one woman too many because two years ago, the last one he was living with shot his balls off and then put three bullets in his chest. Charlie didn't have any family, so the land went up for auction, and I made sure I came out with the highest bid. It cost me a lot of money, but I don't want anything or anyone living here ever again."

Christian blinked fast and cleared his throat. "Makes you feel like you control it and can rewrite the history a little bit, doesn't it?"

Jonah jerked with a tight nod. "Yes."

Nodding too, Christian said, "Yeah, I can understand that."

"Thank you." Jonah's words were rough and breathy, as if he didn't have a drop of saliva in his mouth or throat.

Instinct kicked in again, and this time Christian did not fight it. He slid around Jonah, pushed the man against the front of the truck, and pinned him there with hands on either side of his body. Christian cocked his head to the side and raised a brow. "What's this about being able to buy property, just like that?" His mind raced back to something small Jonah had let slip into his raw confession a few nights ago. It dinged again in Christian's head now. "And did I hear you say something about having employees? You got something more going on aside from being 'just a guy who fixes bikes'? Are you holding out on me, Roberts? Am I getting hard for a *suit?*"

Jonah stared, confusion evident in his eyes. Then he seemed to understand, and the tension eased from his body. Feeling victory, Christian watched a half smile lighten the hard lines on Jonah's face. "Not a suit exactly," Jonah answered. His fingertips drifted down Christian's stomach and found his cock. Two strokes through Christian's jeans had his dick twitching and straining for more. "But you are getting hard for the boss." Redness that had nothing to do with the sun burned Jonah's cheeks. "I own two bike shops, and we do custom cars now too. Both places do all right."

Shit. Everywhere Christian turned or looked, Jonah impressed the hell out of him, proving himself so much more than the sullen teen who'd sparked Christian's early interest in boys or the good man who inched deeper into Christian's already-stolen heart. Jonah struggled so much, when all he really had to do was let go and the world would love him.

Just as much as Christian already—still—did.

As the truth hit Christian, Jonah grabbed hold of Christian's shirt, his grip twisting the fabric. Jonah's pale eyes didn't hold a fleck of cold in them anymore, only intense, naked need. "Make love to me, Christian." His gaze hardened briefly as it slid over Christian's shoulder. After a blink, he came back to Christian. "Right where we stand."

Christian's cock grew, making him groan. "God, baby"— he tunneled his hands in Jonah's hair and drew the man's face down to his—"I'd do that in a heartbeat, believe me." He leaned in and rubbed his ridge against Jonah's equally hard cock. "But I don't have stuff in my car."

"I put the lube in the glove compartment before we left the house." Jonah's face flamed even redder, and he rushed through his confession in a flash. "There's all kinds of hotels and motels between Tampa and Coleman, and when I agreed to come I thought, well, you know, that we might stop on the way home. So if that's your only reason—"

Christian clamped his hand over Jonah's mouth. "That was my only reason." He moved his hand and kissed Jonah once, hard. As he pulled away, he cupped Jonah's cheek and rubbed his thumb across the man's sexy mouth. "Don't move. I'll be right back."

Racing around the front of the truck, Christian yanked the passenger door open and scrambled half onto the seat. His fingers fumbled with the latch on the glove compartment, the excitement at getting to fuck Jonah again turning him into a bundle of nerves. After pinching his skin in the latch twice, Christian finally got it open and grabbed the lube. Damn, he loved the way Jonah planned for a little afternoon quickie. Slamming the glove compartment door hard so that it would catch, Christian backed out, took three strides toward Jonah...and stopped dead two feet away, his breath catching and jamming his throat.

Jonah stood in the exact same spot Christian had left him, but he already had shoes and socks kicked to the side, and his shirt rumpled on the ground too. Jonah's hard, wide chest and fully cut, narrow waist and belly shone with sweat, defining his olive skin and muscles and robbing Christian of speech. The lube fell from Christian's hand as he stared openly, unable to tear his gaze away.

"What?" Stooping quickly, Jonah grabbed his shirt. "Did you change your mind?"

Christian whipped his hand out and grabbed Jonah's wrist, not letting him move that T-shirt an inch closer to his perfect body. He shook Jonah's arm, forcing him to release his fingers and let the material fall to the ground again. With their proximity, Jonah's rich scent sank into Christian, stirring the part of him that believed in mates. His palm burned where he still held Jonah's wrist, and he imagined that he stamped an invisible brand on Jonah, tying the man to him forever.

The feral feeling swirled deeper within, making Christian want to lick, bite, and devour. He wanted to do damage and have Jonah begging for it, the depth of which scared the hell out of Christian. More so than knowing he was in love.

"Christian?" The unsteadiness in Jonah's tone broke through to Christian, and Christian lifted up his gaze.

Questions lurked in the depths of Jonah's eyes, pulling Christian's response out through a scratchy throat. "I have never seen such a thing of beauty as you."

"Shit." Jonah looked away, his Adam's apple bobbing repeatedly as he swallowed. "You're always about two words away from making me come."

Christian grasped Jonah's jaw and drew him back face-to-face. "Then maybe I need to shut up." He fused his mouth to Jonah's, smashing their lips in a hard crush.

Jonah grabbed on tight to Christian's hips and slanted his mouth across Christian's, immediately opening wide and deepening the kiss. Jonah's unending appetite, that he didn't know how to hide, was like alcohol to a flame for Christian, flashing heat all through his body in one fiery blaze. He tore at Jonah's belt buckle and got the button and zipper open too. Pushing his hands inside jeans and underwear to Jonah's hips, Christian moaned at the feel of Jonah's smooth, hard flesh beneath his fingers.

Their tongues tangled in an aggressive tango, with each of them battling to get inside and consume the other. Christian squeezed Jonah's hips and ground their crotches together, but God, his entire being vibrated for a piece of Jonah's ass again. Sliding his hands around under Jonah's clothes, Christian pushed his fingers down to grab hold of Jonah's buttocks and rocked them together some more. He kneaded the taut orbs, pulling them apart as best he could and letting the tips of his fingers slip into Jonah's crack a little more each time. Soon the light touches were more a torment for Christian than a tease for Jonah, and he ripped Jonah's jeans and underwear down to his thighs. Freer now,

Christian pried Jonah's cheeks apart and slid his digits down Jonah's crease, caressing Jonah's tight hole. Jonah bucked and broke the kiss, whimpering as he pushed his ass back into the touch. Aroused as hell himself, Christian did it again, pausing this time to tease the snapped-shut entrance with repeated flicks.

Jonah dropped his head to Christian's shoulder, groaning long and low as he took the light ass play like a guy who had been dreaming about getting fucked forever. Jonah grabbed at the hem of Christian's T-shirt and pulled it up with frantic fingers. "Take off your clothes." He didn't wait for the shirt to clear Christian's head before dipping down and licking a wet line from one of Christian's nipples to the other. "Please. I need to see and feel you too."

They broke contact for a moment, and Jonah shucked his jeans the rest of the way down his legs. Christian got his own shirt off and disposed of his shoes and socks while simultaneously shoving his jeans and underwear down as well. His dark skin shimmered with a bronzy hue, and his dick stuck out hard and straight, already painful with the need to take Jonah's ass again. Two feet away, Jonah's cock reared up toward his belly, and his balls hung heavy, making Christian hungry for them again.

Jonah cleared his throat and dropped to his knees. He looked up, his hands locked into fists at his sides, tearing Christian apart. "I want it here on the ground." Jonah's head started to lower, but, as if he caught himself, he didn't let it happen. "I want you to come in me, on me, and I want you to make me lose it into this grass too."

Christian nodded, his voice escaping him for a few swallows. He circled where Jonah knelt and dropped to his knees behind him, cradling Jonah as best he could with spread thighs and his chest against Jonah's back. Jonah's head did drop this time, and Christian kissed his exposed nape, feeling the corded tendons under his lips, and the shiver that went through Jonah's body. Christian scraped his lips along Jonah's shoulder, the one without the tattoo that he hadn't given proper attention to this morning. Warmth emanated through Jonah's skin, evoking a feeling of safety and home, even in this openly vulnerable state. Christian slid his hands down the sides of Jonah's body, stealing more of that inner heat as he peppered Jonah's shoulder, upper back, and arm with little kisses meant to do nothing more than let Jonah know Christian was here.

As Christian did that, he grazed his palms around to Jonah's stomach and up to his chest, touching over every inch of skin until the abrasion of two pinpoint nipples scraped against the tips of his fingers. He took the hard tips in a pinch, tweaking and tugging, going at Jonah a little roughly until the man inhaled sharply, hissing through his teeth. Christian licked his way to Jonah's ear, murmuring pleased noises as the salty flavor of sweat sprung life to his tongue.

"You like that?" He nipped Jonah's earlobe and pulled on his nipples again, drawing a little gasp.

Jonah clenched his jaw and nodded. "I like everything you do to me."

Smiling, Christian dipped into Jonah's ear and probed with his tongue. "Ditto." He gave Jonah's nipples one more twist and pull, but reluctantly let them go. He would give them full attention another time. Christian sucked on the sensitive skin just below Jonah's ear, pulling blood to the surface. His cock pushed hard against Jonah's backside as he thought about leaving a hickey—something he'd never done to a boy or girl while in high school. Jonah tilted his head to the side, giving Christian complete access, and even sighed at the teenage move.

Not wanting to let up even for a second, Christian felt around in the grass in small circles, searching for the lube. After just a few tries, his fingers brushed against soft plastic, and he scooped it up. He popped the lid with his thumbnail, brought it between their bodies, and squeezed a dollop onto two fingers. Jonah's body rested on his heels, preventing Christian from sliding his fingers where he desperately wanted them to go. "Ease up a bit, baby. Let me have your ass."

Jonah did more than rise to his knees; he shifted forward and planted his shoulders into the ground, and dug his cheek there as well. He spread his bent legs wide under and on either side of him and, in the process, split his cheeks apart and exposed his dark hole. "I'm so hard for you, Christian." Jonah's voice reverberated into the ground. "Take me and make me come."

Jonah's bud sat there snug, small, and pulsing as if it had its own heartbeat, and Christian's cock beat with blood in kind. Christian wanted to give Jonah everything he requested, everything he seemed to *need*, so he ignored his own leaking prick and leaned in, rubbing his lubed fingers against Jonah's pucker instead.

A shocked noise escaped Jonah, and he arched his back. "More." He pushed back into Christian's touch, wiggling his ass. "Give me more."

Christian spread an open palm on the small of Jonah's back, holding him in place, and lined the tip of one finger against Jonah's ring. "Take a breath and push back," Christian instructed as he started to bear down on the tight barrier. "Right"—he increased the pressure—"now."

Opposing forces shoved at the same time, and with one hard jam, Christian broke through and invaded Jonah's ass. Jonah cried out as his entrance closed around Christian's digit, and his channel sucked the length more than halfway inside his scorching tunnel. Heat burned a singe mark around Christian's buried finger, but he didn't waste a moment and quickly forced a second finger through, widening Jonah's ring and tight chute.

"Move on my fingers, Jonah." Christian pulled almost all the way out but, right before getting there, pushed his way back inside. "Let me fuck you this way and help you come." Jonah's passage rippled all around Christian's sheathed fingers and clenched at him at the same time. Jonah wanted it; he wanted it so badly. Christian could feel it. "Fucking lose it and spray your seed into the ground. For me." *For yourself.*

"'Kay." Jonah nodded his head against the grass and worked his ass up and back, grinding on Christian's invasion and then withdrawing, grunting each time Christian pushed his fingers in and took Jonah's ass to the hilt. With only a few thrusts, Jonah's hips and ass grew wild with motion, his body seemingly frantic for the fucking. Christian watched his fingers disappear in and out of Jonah's stretched asshole and listened to the guttural sounds escaping Jonah with every deep plunge. Christian bit back a curse as his cock and balls tingled with the need to take over for his fingers and give Jonah the fucking of his life.

Not yet.

Right then, Jonah rose up on his elbows, jammed his backside into Christian's fingers, and circled, working himself off. "More." Jonah's head hung low, sweat plastered his hair to his scalp, and his muscles flexed and strained, exciting Christian to painful heights. His voice low and hoarse, Jonah uttered, "Give me more."

His insides screaming with need, Christian ignored his erection and covered Jonah, as if he were fucking him with his dick. He pushed a third finger into Jonah's rectum, and with his other hand, he reached under Jonah and grabbed his cock. He pumped into Jonah from behind and started a rough jerking on his rock-hard prick at the same time. Christian crooked his fingers inside Jonah, going right for the kill zone, and began an all-out assault.

It was like a bolt of lightning shot right through Jonah's spine, and he jerked as if the resulting electricity raced all through him. Christian didn't let up on Jonah's sweet spot, and he milked Jonah's prick just as hard, taking a few seconds to torture his balls with a rough tug before going right back to his dick, stroking it from base to tip and then rimming the sensitive head. Jonah's hips moved frantically back and forth under Christian, as if his body struggled to know which pleasure to reach for the most. Jonah whimpered, and his ass squeezed down on Christian's fingers, his desperate need clear.

Christian guided the head of Jonah's cock right into the ground and gave him the final step. He flicked the wide, leaking slit and whispered at Jonah's ear, "Come."

In near silence, Jonah buried his face in the grass and released. The smallest noise escaped him as his body heaved and his member thickened in Christian's hand. Warm cum spilled into the earth, saturating this one spot with a dozen little pulses, ones that matched the contractions in his ass, strong at first, and then each one slightly lighter until they eventually stopped.

Knowing this single act wasn't enough, Christian let go of Jonah's penis and withdrew his fingers from Jonah's rectum. Christian paused to press a kiss against the center of Jonah's back, letting his lips caress and linger, and then shifted to Jonah's side and lay down, flat on his back. He reached out and turned Jonah's head, forcing eye contact. The shakiness there almost undid Christian but also reiterated that they weren't finished with this afternoon yet. "Now ride me." Without looking away, Christian found the open lube and slicked up his own cock. "You control it this time, Jonah, and make it happen again."

No words were spoken aloud, but the raw, stripped-down expression on Jonah's face spoke a thousand confessions. Jonah stared as he crawled on top of Christian and straddled his lap and cock. He reached around his body, took Christian's rigid penis in hand, and sank down on it in one slow motion, completely sheathing Christian's cock.

Christian bit back a groan of pleasure along with an order for Jonah to move fast, and he let Jonah set the pace. Jonah leaned back, planted his hands on Christian's knees, and started to undulate his hips in a whisper-soft motion, driving Christian to complete distraction. Christian's cock sat lodged in Jonah's anus, the most wonderful suffocating heat wrapping him up tight, when all Christian's hard dick wanted was friction, friction, and more friction. Christian's pubes scratched at Jonah's hole and crack, and the picture that flashed in Christian's head—that he sat buried so deeply inside Jonah—had Christian moaning and his prick swelling, pushing at Jonah's snug walls. Jonah's eyes widened, and his channel clenched twice, hard and fast, drawing gasps out of both men. Shockingly, Jonah's cock began to stir, rising again.

Jonah abruptly shifted his hold from Christian's knees to Christian's torso, the heels of his hands digging in with bruising force. "Touch yourself," Jonah ordered, his voice rough. "Play with your nipples the same as you did mine."

Excitement coursed through Christian, and he could see a new flash of fire lighting Jonah's eyes. Christian stared at Jonah while he licked the pads of his thumbs and rubbed them around his nipples, getting them wet. Jonah's gaze dropped to Christian's hands and chest, and with Christian's first tug on his hard tips, Jonah lifted off Christian's cock and sank right back down, enveloping his length again and getting them moving.

Christian's dick cried with joy. Jonah pulled up and then bore back down, one agonizing inch at a time, the skin on his face turning ruddy as Christian's cock forced Jonah's channel to widen for him again. Every bit of Jonah's unpracticed moves had Christian nearly spending himself right there. The pleasure went so deep it raced into his belly and up his spine, and even started rising the hairs on his arms and legs. Christian pinched his nipples and pulled the skin even harder, the light pain nearly as sweet as watching Jonah learn to find his own pleasure, one stroke at a time.

Jonah picked up the pace with agonizing slowness, but eventually his face contorted and he had trouble catching his breath. His slides up and down Christian's erection grew erratic and became something more of a repeated slamming of his hips in a fast frenzy, sending the nerve endings in Christian's cock into a blazing inferno. Christian couldn't help himself; he grabbed Jonah's hips and speared up into his ass, filling him to the root and taking a little bit of control.

Jonah's dick jumped to full attention and captured Christian's interest, a dark, beautiful male thing that Christian couldn't wait to get his mouth around again. Jonah reached down and took himself in hand, wrapping his member in a tight fist and pulling so hard he made himself cry out. Jonah didn't stop or even slow down, though, and in fact jerked himself off harder with piston-fast strokes that nearly matched the pace Christian took over in his ass.

A low moan rumbled up from deep within Jonah, and he looked to be in near agony of needing to come. Christian knew the feeling. He dug the back of his head into the ground and bit his cheek, drawing blood, fighting off orgasm with everything in him. Christian's balls sucked up painfully tight to his body, though, fighting against his determination not to come.

Jonah looked at Christian, and through the haze of lust, clarity broke through. "Let go," Jonah pleaded, his voice barely sounding human. "Let me feel you. Please."

He didn't even get the "please" out before Christian plunged deep into Jonah's ass one final time and shot, keening as the floodgates opened and he let go of everything, filling Jonah's hole with cum.

The first spit hit, and Jonah cried out too, his anus clamping like a vise on Christian's cock. Jonah pumped his erection in his fist and released a stream of ejaculate all over Christian, splashing semen on Christian's skin in a thick, milky shower that coated Christian's chest and branded his heart.

Jonah panted above Christian, looking as exhausted as if he had just run a marathon. *Perhaps in his mind, he has.* Making sure Jonah was watching, Christian wiped his hand through the seed covering his chest and smeared his hand into the grass at his side, giving it a piece of Jonah's new life essence, praying that it would drown the old. When he did that, he reached up and pulled Jonah down to him, pressing a reassuring kiss to his lips, lingering there without voraciousness, just connection.

Eventually, Jonah's lips lost their tension, and he kissed Christian back, settling some of Christian's concerns. Jonah rolled to his side, taking Christian with him. Christian's cock slid out of Jonah's ass, but their arms and legs remained tangled, and Jonah rested his chin on top of Christian's head.

A shaky sigh escaped Jonah, rustling Christian's hair. "I didn't do this to desecrate or dishonor this property or to piss all over my childhood." Jonah paused, clutching Christian to him in a tight hold. "I just wanted to have a new memory for when I close my eyes and dream about this place."

Christian held Jonah just as hard, maybe too hard, but somehow knew he needed it. He kissed Jonah's shoulder and tucked his face into the crook of his neck. "I know," he said against Jonah's warm skin. "I know."

Jonah squeezed and nuzzled his cheek against Christian's hair. "I want to lie here and think for a little while right now, before we go home, if that's okay?"

Christian would happily give Jonah all the time, sex...love he needed. Right now, though, he just said, "Take as long as you need," and settled in for a nap.

Chapter Thirteen

Jonah pulled Christian up the porch steps, laughing at the way Christian dragged his feet. "Come on, man." He tugged Christian to him and wrapped his arms around the other man's waist. "You can't seriously be that tired."

"Must be the nap and the sun." Yawning, Christian leaned against Jonah while Jonah unlocked the door. "I can barely keep my eyes open."

After their stop, and seeing Christian's lethargy upon waking up, Jonah had taken over driving the rest of the way to Coleman. Jonah didn't mind trading off or the relative quiet; it all felt very *partner-y*. Jonah grinned, relief washing through him that he could still smile. He'd revealed so much to Christian today, things he had never told or shown to another soul. While holding Christian in that field—funnily enough while Christian napped and Jonah lay awake—he began to worry that he had given Christian too much and would kill any sense of comfort they'd managed to build over the last week, particularly the last few days. So far, though, they seemed okay.

The next thirty seconds would test just how many liberties Jonah could take in this *partnership* with Christian.

Jonah threaded his fingers in Christian's, pushed open the door, and led the man inside.

Christian took one step, and his sneakers squeaked to a halt. "Holy shit." Clearly wide-awake now, Christian scanned the living room, and Jonah held his breath. Christian absorbed the newly installed hardwood flooring, along with the dark baseboards that had also been put in place today. The wood gleamed under the overhead lights, also new fixtures. The final touch in this room: a cream-colored contemporary design sofa and a leather-covered coffee table. After taking another sweeping glance, Christian looked up at Jonah, complete puzzlement widening his dark eyes.

"Happy birthday," Jonah said, although, Christ, with his sudden case of nerves it came out as more of a rough whisper.

Two lines of shadows appeared on the new flooring, and a second later Rodrigo and Abby appeared from the direction of the kitchen. "Surprise," Abby said, smiling. "Hope you like it. We didn't take the day off after all. We also had a little bit of help."

"Some of the guys from the crew stepped in for the day to lend a hand," Rodrigo shared. "They said to give you their best and to tell you they want to see your ass back on the job soon."

Christian looked from Abby, to Rodrigo, to the floors, and finally back to Jonah. "What?" Complete confusion still laced his voice.

Jonah's muscles tensed, and he suddenly wished he didn't have an audience. "Rodrigo pulled me outside the other day to tell me that it was your birthday today."

"I didn't even think about it," Christian answered.

"That's what we figured," Jonah said. He had wondered if Christian's mother would remember her son's special day; with Christian's shock and his comment, Jonah now concluded she definitely hadn't.

Rodrigo moved a step forward. "I asked Jonah what he thought we should do about it, or if we should even mention it. He came up with the idea of going ahead and laying the hardwood flooring while you were gone today as a surprise."

"Because I remembered you mentioning that you weren't looking forward to that," Jonah quickly explained. "You had said that was your least favorite thing to do on job sites. There are still the cabinets and counters in the kitchen to reface and replace, and the tile to lay in there and the back of the house, and the porch to be replaced too. I wasn't trying to take over; I just wanted to give you a birthday present, but I didn't know what else to give you."

Christian flinched. "And the stuff today?" He glanced Rodrigo and Abby's way but came back to Jonah. "You know... Was that just to keep me away?"

Jonah jerked, feeling punched in the gut. "That was real, Christian." Fuck, how could he even question that? "It happened because I needed to go there, and I wanted to do it with you. It didn't have anything to do with this."

"Quit being an ass, Chris," Rodrigo said sharply. "We've been done with this for hours. We each even went home to shower and change, and have since been hanging around waiting for you guys to return. Whatever you're talking about, Jonah didn't have to keep you away as long as he did."

"No, Rodrigo," Jonah interrupted, lifting a hand, "it's okay." Damn it, he had second-guessed this a million times in the last two days and *knew* he should have called Rodrigo to cancel. "Christian was clear about his wishes for the work here, and I shouldn't have overst—"

Christian threw himself at Jonah and wrapped his arms around Jonah's waist, shutting him up. "Thank you." He looked up, letting their gazes meet. "I'm sorry. I was just shocked for a minute; that's all. My back, knees, and I all thank you for coming up with this idea. It's a very thoughtful gift."

His heart racing, Jonah dipped down and put his mouth against Christian's ear. "I think I would give you anything, Christian"—his quiet words rocked through both of them— "if I only knew what was right."

Christian took a step back but kept one hand on Jonah's waist. "I couldn't ask for more than today." His gaze held Jonah's, conveying a dozen more sentences behind that one. "All of it." He brushed his hand against Jonah's jaw.

Jonah grabbed Christian's hand, held it close, and pressed a kiss to his palm. "Happy birthday, from all of us." He included Rodrigo and Abby. "I'm glad you like it." He lowered their hands between them but didn't let Christian's go. "Want to see the other rooms?"

"Sure." Christian jerked a thumb toward the new furniture first. "But what's with the couch and coffee table?"

Abby raised her hand. "That's my contribution. You don't want a lot of furniture in a house you're trying to sell, but one or two pieces so that it doesn't look like an empty cave is a good thing." She smiled and shrugged. "I saw it on HGTV. Come." She crooked her finger and opened the door to the first bedroom, flicking on the light switch. "Take a look at the two other pieces I bought."

Only having heard about Abby's plan to purchase a few things, but not having seen anything in person, Jonah peeked into the room, just as in the dark as Christian. A queen-size bed—had to be, a king would take over the space—with a deep brown, stitched leather headboard sat center against one wall, fully dressed out in crisp bedding done in whites and tans. A bench sat butted up against the foot of the bed, covered in a camel material, a perfect match for the bed in length and size. When paired with the new dark flooring and the cool, clean walls, the room had the beginnings of a very cozy space.

"It's beautiful," Christian murmured. "What are you going to do with it, and the other stuff, when the house sells?"

"Don't worry about that." Abby waved a hand. "If the new owners don't want it, then I can always find a friend who will take it off my hands. I got it dirt cheap from a client I have a good relationship with. He's a good guy." She slid Rodrigo a quick look that held muted fire. "We all have our connections and uses."

Rodrigo just blinked, as if bored, and shifted his focus to Christian. "You want to see the other rooms?" He didn't wait for an answer but rather started moving, and the rest followed. Only a little over a week knowing the guy, and Jonah knew Rodrigo simply expected everyone to follow.

The entire front of the house, from the living room, to the dining room, the long pass-through hallway, and four bedrooms all flowed with the same hardwood flooring, all complete and beautifully done. Rodrigo, Abby, and the others had even pulled the beds and bookshelf out of Jonah and Christian's room and not only did the floor, but painted the walls to match the rest of the house. The mattress on the floor had been very nice for a few days—especially since he shared it with Christian—but maybe they could try out that new bed tonight.

Thank you, Abby.

Jonah wondered how long it would take him to get Rodrigo and Abby out of the house—and if Christian would welcome a birthday fucking to end their day.

Rodrigo completed the tour in the kitchen, after spending considerable time in each room one-upping Abby's stories about the work done today.

"We'll lay sheets down until we're finished with the house," Rodrigo said. "But that's just a precaution; we'll bring the rest of the stuff in through the kitchen or the back door. There should be no risk of damage." Rodrigo laid out his plan for the next few days in detail, and Jonah caught Christian biting down a smile as Abby shot him an "oh, geez" look and nearly rolled her eyes. Rodrigo did like to explain how things were going to work, no doubt about it. Jonah had asked Christian about it after the first day of renovations, and Christian explained that the man often repeated himself, purely because he wanted the work done right, the first time. He said the guys on the job were used to it. Clearly, Abby was not.

Jonah watched Christian, and his heart started skipping beats all over again. Fuck. How did he go from feeling virtually nothing for thirty-one years to meeting a man he not only craved sexually, but also struggled to contain *too many* emotions for, all at once?

You always did have too many feelings for Christian, Roberts; you just couldn't understand what they were or have an idea how to unlock them at the time.

Now...maybe now Jonah was ready to try.

Knock, knock, knock.

"Hello? Anyone home?" A masculine voice broke through, strong enough to stop even Rodrigo midsentence. "It's Braden." The man gave name to voice. "You have a door open up here." Braden appeared in the kitchen seconds later, clearly having let himself inside. He found Christian in the small group. "That's not really a good idea. I just closed and locked it for you."

"Thank you," Christian answered. Any sense of lightness that shone in Christian just a moment ago disappeared in a flash before Jonah's eyes, and tight lines formed around his mouth. "Detective, you remember Jonah. This is Rodrigo Santiago and Abby Gaines." He pointed each out. "They've been helping with a lot of the renovations on the house."

Braden stuck his hand out to Rodrigo first. "Good to meet you." He received a handshake and a murmur in kind from Rodrigo and then turned to Abby. "Nice to meet you too." He extended the same quick, firm-looking clasp of hands to Abby as he did for Rodrigo before turning back to Christian. "Looks like you've done a hell of a lot of work in just a few days. Congratulations."

"Not me." Christian shook his head. "Rodrigo, Abby, and a few other guys did the floors today."

"As a birthday gift," Abby added. "It's Chris's today."

"Happy birthday." Braden dipped his head in acknowledgment.

Christian's smile looked forced. "Thank you."

Jonah couldn't stand to see the strain in Christian and moved in right at his side, facing Braden square-on. "Christian is being polite, but I don't give a shit what you think about me. What are you doing here, Crenshaw? What have you learned?"

Braden didn't so much as fidget under Jonah's raised voice. He looked to Rodrigo and Abby and then came back to Christian.

"It's okay." Christian answered the question in Braden's eyes. "Rodrigo and Abby pretty much know everything. Rodrigo is my boss and friend, and Abby is a good friend. They know I talked to you and what it was about."

"All right, I'll cut right to the chase then." Braden leaned against the counter and crossed his arms. "I don't like what I see in David. At the very least, with your permission, I'm going to sell your need for a restraining order as hard as I can. I am also going to contact the DA's office and see if there's any charge you can file against David they would be open to prosecuting. I still don't know that I'm going to be successful with either avenue, so I want you to be careful when David comes into your path. I believe he eventually will again. I don't think we should mess around here. I'm going to agree with Jonah and say I think this guy could become dangerous."

Cold fear sliced through Jonah. He moved in behind Christian and pulled the man in against his chest, as if he could protect Christian forever by keeping them glued together. "What the hell did David say to you that turned you around so quickly?"

Rodrigo and Abby moved in too, each taking a stance at Christian's sides, flanking him.

"Explain yourself, Detective," Rodrigo said, his voice hard. "I don't like fear tactics used on my friends without reason. You'd better have one, and if you do, you'd better fucking be prepared to tell us what you intend to do to protect Christian."

Once again, Braden Crenshaw delivered a cool stare to Rodrigo but then shifted his focus and dealt with Christian. "Were you aware that David still has his old apartment? That he didn't give up the lease when he got married and moved into his wife's residence?"

"No," Christian answered. "But like I told you, once I started coming out, we never really met anywhere that would reflect on him. I didn't spend a lot of time in his apartment, not even in the beginning. Is it relevant?"

"It's a strong indication that he always intended to keep living two lives," Braden said. "He rents it, so it's not an investment he has any financial incentive to keep. He resigned the lease five months ago."

"Shit." Christian wiped his mouth, his hand trembling.

Jonah rubbed Christian's arms, feeling the chill in him. He tried to offer some kind of comfort even though his hands felt completely tied.

"Did you talk to him?" Christian asked.

"I did," Braden confirmed. "I kept it very open and cordial. I let him know you and I are friends, and that as your friend you expressed some concern to me about his behavior, and that if it didn't stop, you wanted to know what your rights were and what kind of steps you could take to make sure it does stop. He acted like he didn't know what I was talking about, which is to be expected. I shared a few details with him about our conversation. When he started recognizing specifics, he gave me his full attention. I assured him I wasn't out to ruin his life, but that if he chose to keep pursuing contact with you there would be consequences and they would become a matter of public record, well beyond my control. That sobered him, and I think he's going to spend some time thinking about it."

Christian straightened. "It sounds like you got through to him. That's exactly what I hoped would happen. He fears exposure. He'll back off now."

Jonah absorbed Braden's sober tone and face and didn't like the knot that twisted in his stomach. He held Christian even closer against his front. "You don't think it's gonna stick," he said to Braden. "Tell us why."

Finally, Braden lifted his focus to Jonah and spoke directly to him. "I also took a look in David's car while we chatted," he explained. "Just through the window, very subtle. I noticed a lot of cigarette stubs in the ashtray, fast-food bags, coffee cups...stuff like that. That caught my attention. Based on how Christian described David, I expected more of a neat-freak perfectionist. That's also what

I would have expected based on his appearance and the way he carries himself."

"Don't know about neat freak," Christian said, "but he's definitely not a slob."

"That was my read too," Braden said. "So here's the deal: David is clearly spending a lot of time in his car. Since his phone call to you implied he was aware of whatever you two have going"—Braden shifted eye contact between Christian and Jonah—"my money says he's spending that time following you, watching you. Pair that with the apartment and the encounters and the last phone call..."

"And your gut," Jonah said it for him. "You met David and something in your gut said he's potentially dangerous, and you can't ignore that, no matter what. Right?"

Braden nodded. "Correct."

Shivering, Christian pulled out of Jonah's hold. He rubbed his arms and slid into one of the chairs at the kitchen table. Facing no one, as if talking to himself, he said, "So then why didn't I see it? I spent a ton of time with him and never saw anything that would foreshadow this."

Abby stepped in before Jonah could, pressed a kiss to the top of Christian's head, and rubbed his shoulder. "I met him too, Chris, more than once, and I didn't see it either."

"I didn't either," Rodrigo said. The man didn't close ranks like Abby did, but Jonah could see the helpless desire to do *something* in Rodrigo's pained expression. Fuck, Jonah understood that: the helplessness. "And I'd put my ability to judge a person's character up against anyone's, any day of the week. You don't have anything to feel foolish about here. Understand?"

"Yeah," Abby agreed. She glanced at Rodrigo and gave him a nod and a small smile. "It's Detective Crenshaw's job to see something others don't. And Jonah—" Her mouth snapped shut, and her face burned as she sneaked a peek at Braden before looking back at Jonah. "Well…"

"I had years to study nothing but criminals while I was in juvenile detention." Jonah easily read Abby's mind. "It's okay, you can say it." Jonah slid a knowing glance in Braden's direction. "I'm sure Detective Crenshaw has already looked me up."

Braden nodded. "It's part of my job to know as much as I can. You don't have anything on your adult record. I've got no issue with you."

Rodrigo's jaw clenched, and he moved a few steps in on Braden. Braden's pupils flared, and he looked Rodrigo up and down, but other than that, it didn't look like he so much as breathed.

"You have something you want to get off your chest, Mr. Santiago?" Braden asked, his voice eerily calm.

"Damn straight I do." Rodrigo looked like he wanted to lean in and intimidate, claim some space, but Jonah knew by now the man was too smart to push around a law enforcement officer. "You have plenty of warnings and gut instincts for my friend, but I don't hear anything about answers. You come in here and scare people really well, but I don't hear a lot about helping so that Christian doesn't have to be scared to death every time he leaves the house."

"Leave him alone, Rodrigo." Christian's voice sliced across the room. "This isn't his fault."

Jonah whirled on Christian, swooping right in on him. "And it's not yours either." He took Christian's chin in hand and forced him to make eye contact. The moisture, the pure *sadness* there, nearly killed Jonah. "You don't think it is, do you?"

"No, I don't." The solid strength in Christian's voice backed up the words. "But I'm also not happy that someone else has confirmed this same bad gut feeling that you have. Whatever his damage, David is a human being. I can't feel good that his life is going to be destroyed. I'm sorry, but I can't."

Jonah flinched and pulled back, letting his hand drop from Christian's jaw. "I'm not asking you to be."

"Of course he's not," Abby said. "Nobody is. Detective—" She lifted her gaze, stumbled on Rodrigo first, who still stood in front of Braden, and then shifted until she looked into Braden's eyes. "Is there anything you can do, or even we can do, unofficially, to take care of this without turning David's life into a public spectacle?"

"Call me Braden, please." Braden put that intense focus of his on Abby, and she rubbed her hand over the back of her neck. Jonah noticed it, and he noticed Rodrigo notice it too. Once again, though, Braden moved to the kitchen table, took the seat opposite Christian, and spoke directly to him. "I can't arrest David right now anyway; I don't have anything to hold him on. This isn't going to blow up in his face tomorrow. It doesn't ever have to; it's entirely up to him. He has choices to make, and what we can hope is that he makes the right ones. After I talk to someone in the DA's office, I'll have a better sense of what our options are. When I do, if you'd like, I can talk to David again and give him more proof that he really needs to end this harassment now. Having said that, I have a PI friend who owes me a favor. I can ask him to keep a watch on David for a while, just to see what he's doing. It's possible that David will slink away and go back to his new life with his wife. I am not one hundred percent certain of anything; assumptions like that will get you into trouble every time. I can tell you that I'd feel more comfortable if you had someone with you when you go out, at least until I can gather some more information and we can formulate a better plan. Right now, this is just informal, unofficial information between friends. Okay?"

Christian's gaze dropped to the table. Jonah watched, his muscles tense, as Christian scratched a nick into the surface with the edge of his chewed-down thumbnail. "I know I have to do something," Christian said, his voice soft. "I'm not stupid or ignorant about my own safety. I just don't like that I have to do it. It doesn't feel good."

"I understand that. Look at me for a minute here, Chris." Braden reached across the table and covered Christian's hand with his, drawing his attention up from the table. "I never feel good about arresting someone and altering his or her life forever, but sometimes it has to be done for the greater safety of others. If I'm able to get a restraining order, my professional advice is that you let me issue it, for your safety. Nothing's going to make you feel good about it, and I won't either, but my belief is that it needs to be done."

Christian studied Braden, looking like he was taking his measure, for an excruciating dragged-out minute. "All right," Christian said, and Jonah started breathing again. "Do it."

Thank you, Braden Crenshaw.

"Keep me informed," Christian added.

Braden squeezed Christian's hand. "Will do." He released the hold and stood. "I'll let myself out."

"Wait!" Abby grabbed Braden's arm but quickly snatched her hand away. "Sorry about that."

Braden looked at his forearm, where Abby had touched him. He shook his head and looked up. "It's all right. What did you need?"

"You really brought this room down, Detective Crenshaw," Abby informed him. "Totally killed the vibe we had going. So now you have to join us for dinner and help lift it back up. It's Christian's birthday, and we are not ending the day on this sour note."

"That's kind of you." Braden glanced around the small group. "But—"

"Yes, it is kind of me." Abby talked over Braden's protest. "And you're going to be equally kind and accept."

Rodrigo moved in, edging Braden out of eye contact. "Damn it, woman, if the man doesn't want to join us, then let him leave."

"Zip it, Santiago." Abby pointed right in his face. "For once, you are not running the show."

A flare of visible heat burned in Rodrigo's dark eyes. "I warned you about that finger."

Christian rubbed at the furrow between his brows. "Guys."

Abby clamped her hand over Christian's mouth. "Nope, I don't want to hear it. You obviously had a great day with

Jonah, you liked your birthday present, and damn it, you're going to let me and Rodrigo treat you to a nice meal with your friends and love the hell out of that too. I don't want to hear another word about it." She moved around the table and hauled Christian and Jonah to their feet. "You guys go shower and change. Double up and make it fast." She smacked each of them on the ass and got them moving. "You've got ten minutes, and the clock is ticking."

Jonah followed Christian to their room, wondering how the hell this day had turned so completely, yet again. He didn't want food; he wanted to be in that new bed with Christian. Holding him, making sure he was safe. Jonah watched as Christian gathered a change of clothes, but stopped him before he could exit the room. "Are you okay?" Cupping Christian's neck, Jonah rubbed his thumb under Christian's jaw. "If you're not up to it, we don't have to go."

His lips still a little pale, Christian shrugged. "I'm all right." It took a moment, but a small smile did eventually appear. "Truth is, I can probably use the distraction. It'll be interesting to watch Braden observe Rodrigo and Abby bickering, if nothing else."

Not sure what to do, Jonah eased up his worry and followed Christian's lead. "You could be right." He leaned in and pecked a kiss on Christian's temple, grabbed his own clothes, and tucked them under his arm. "Let's go get that shower before we get in trouble."

* * *

Fifteen minutes later, everyone filed out through the front door, pausing on the porch long enough for Jonah to lock the knob and bolt.

Inside the house, another door *snicked.* The closet door in the first bedroom opened just as the bolt on the front door slid home. The man inside wandered the home, navigating through the shadows.

The occasional slash of moon and streetlights cut through the darkness, reflecting off the metal of the gun in his hand.

Chapter Fourteen

Christian slipped in behind Jonah as Jonah unlocked the front door. "This is familiar." He leaned up and nipped the back of Jonah's neck, getting a secret thrill at the very nice love bite marring the man's skin under his ear. "Got any more surprises behind door number one that I should know about?"

Jonah reached back and rubbed his hand down Christian's thigh. "Not a one. You sound like you're smiling." He jiggled the key and finally got the finicky bolt to turn. "It's nice."

Christian almost melted, but at the same time, he felt about ten feet taller. Sweet Jonah, the man had no idea how sensitive and in tune with the world he was. Well, with Christian anyway. "I am smiling. I have to admit that Abby was right; I needed to get out with friends. I do feel better."

Jonah worked the key in the knob's lock, and the door slid open. He reached in and flipped the light switch, then turned in Christian's arms. "Sure it wasn't my bike making you feel better?" He hooked two fingers into the waist of Christian's jeans and tugged him over the threshold. Stopping to kick the door closed, he looked down at Christian's cock and smiled. "That's a hell of a lot of vibration between your legs if you've never straddled a bike out on the open road before." Rodrigo, Abby, and Braden had each driven their own cars so they could head straight home after dinner. For the first time since coming into town, Jonah had offered to put Christian on the back of his bike for a ride.

Jonah was right. The power, vibrations, and being able to hold on to Jonah had been incredible.

But that didn't even begin to come close to the half wood Christian sported through dinner, the entire ride home—and still did—all because Jonah had slipped his hand into Christian's while they waited outside the restaurant for a table. *Out in public.* Where the large group of people also waiting to eat could see them.

Holy. Shit.

"Christian?" Jonah yanked on Christian's jeans, bringing him to the present. "You okay?"

"Better than." Christian snaked his arm around Jonah's neck and pulled him down until their noses touched. "Take me to bed"—he teased the seam of Jonah's lips with his tongue, darting quickly to the heat inside—"and I'll show you."

Jonah raised a brow. "You thinking what I've been thinking all night?"

Christian glanced toward the hall in the direction of the bedrooms. "Try out the new one?"

Jonah's hand slipped around Christian's waist to his ass. Drawing him close, he said, "You got it in one."

"Thank you, Abby."

Jonah chuckled. "Said the very same thing to myself a little bit ago." Walking backward and pulling Christian with him, Jonah dipped down and stole another kiss, then stayed there, nibbling on Christian's sensitized lips. "Open up, honey," he whispered against Christian's mouth. Just as Christian did and their tongues brushed, a loud *crack!* rent the air. Jonah grunted, and his full weight fell into Christian, making Christian cry out as he stumbled and they fell to the floor.

Wham! Another thudding hit jarred through Jonah and into Christian. Jonah slumped off Christian's body into a heap on the floor.

"Jonah!"

"Don't help him." David's voice, so coldly calm, cut through Christian like sleet on a freezing morning. Snatching his hand back, automatically obeying, Christian looked up and found David a few feet away with a two-by-four swinging in his hands. He looked the same as a thousand other times Christian had seen him, wearing tan pants and a button-down shirt, his blond hair neat and combed, his face as handsome as Christian ever remembered it.

Except for his eyes, which didn't look quite right.

Christian swallowed, his stomach twisting so completely it wanted to force up his dinner.

David tossed the two-by-four aside, well beyond a distance Christian could reach himself. Before Christian could blink, David reached behind his back, produced a gun, and trained it right on Christian's chest. "Tape him up," David said, his voice inflecting more of that eerie calm. "I found the duct tape; I put it right there by the wall." They stood in the hallway, the open dining room to their left. David pointed toward the front dining area wall with his weapon. "Tape him up good, both his hands and his feet. I don't intend to hurt him, but I swear to God if I see you trying to pull something funny, I will do it so that he's not a problem. Tape him up tight and cover his mouth too. I don't want him yelling down the house if he wakes up."

Christian edged toward the tape, his heart beating faster than it ever had and his stomach churning so hard he thought he might pass out. He knelt down and picked up the tape, and then crawled to Jonah, who still lay motionless on the ground. A trickle of blood flowed down Jonah's neck, marring the white collar of his T-shirt. *Oh, God, Jonah, please be okay.*

Taking a breath, digging deep for steadiness, Christian looked up and made eye contact with David. "Can I check and see if he's still alive?" Christian curled his hand around the roll of tape so that he didn't reach out to search for Jonah's pulse and possibly get them both killed. "Please, David. That's all I ask."

David shook his head and waved his gun again. "Do what I told you." His eyes possessed a pinpoint focus, making them nearly pure blue in a way Christian had never witnessed before. "If you stall a second longer, I'll shoot him and you won't have to worry about it."

"No, please. I'll do what you say." *One thing at a time, Christian, focus on one thing at a time. Do what he wants and take his interest off Jonah.* Christian made quick work of taping up Jonah's wrists and ankles, leaving no room for him to wiggle free, should he stir. Christian tried not to dwell on the fact that Jonah hadn't moved at all; he had to clear his mind of Jonah altogether. He could not afford a single mistake.

"Okay." Christian rose to his feet, his hands outstretched, his focus glued on David and his gun. "What do you want me to do now?"

David circled around Jonah's prone body and jammed his weapon between Christian's shoulder blades. "Ge-get away from him. Walk to the bedroom." Christian blinked, schooling his features not to react to that first hint of weakness. "The one where you let him fuck you."

Christian's legs went wobbly for a moment, but he steadied himself as he moved into the bedroom. His hands still outstretched, he faced away from David, listening as the door clicked shut and the simple knob lock tumbled into place. Light suddenly flooded the room, and Christian blinked a half dozen times while his eyes adjusted to the brightness. His chest hammered hard and fast, and it burned his lungs to breathe normally.

Ignoring the pain, Christian turned around and found David standing at the foot of Jonah's bed, his weapon still aimed at Christian. "How did you get into the house?" Christian scrambled, unable to think much beyond keeping David's mind off Jonah in the hallway, and off Christian and Jonah as a couple. "*I*," he lied, "locked it up tight before I left."

"You shouldn't leave your front door wide open, even for a moment," David answered. His lips thinned and turned hard, and soon his entire face mottled with red. "Detective Crenshaw was right about that."

Shit.

One lapse and here they now stood.

"Then you clearly didn't plan this." Christian latched onto something—anything—to get David talking. "You saw an opportunity, acted on impulse, and slipped inside." He looked into David's eyes, searching for the teenager who had befriended Christian, or the man he once cared about very deeply. A hint of softening dilated David's pupils, giving Christian a glimpse of the David he knew. "You don't want to do this, David. I know you don't." His focus dropped to the gun, and the hands—hands Christian knew could be achingly gentle—wrapped around it. "This is not who you are."

A spark of familiar cockiness lit David's eyes. "You don't think I know how to shoot this gun?"

"I know you can." David's father was a serious hunter and had taken David with him from a very young age. Christian had no idea how he managed to suppress his shudder. He swallowed, searching for saliva and a voice. He moved his attention off the weapon and put it back on David's eyes. "I don't believe you want to use it, though. You're hurt and confused right now, and I'm sorry you're struggling, but this is not the answer, and you know it. You don't want to hurt me; I know you don't."

"Oh, you think I'm here to hurt you?" A funny, frightening laugh escaped David, drenching Christian in an entirely new level of fear. "I'm not." In a flash, he pulled his aim off Christian and put the gun to his own temple. "I'm here to kill myself."

Oh God. Christian closed his eyes, his stomach plummeting, and his legs barely holding him upright.

"Open your eyes!" David snapped, his voice rising with every word. "You have to watch!"

Inhaling deeply, Christian lifted his downturned head and once again met the frantic darting in David's eyes. Christian stripped away everything that had gone down in the last year and talked to the David he used to know. "Please don't kill yourself, David." Christian's chest constricted, aching just saying the words. "You said you weren't here to hurt me, and if you did that, it would hurt me a great deal. I don't want you to die. I just want you to let me get you some help."

"What help?" David's hand grew a little less steady, and his face began to crumble. "The kind of help Detective Crenshaw will offer me? Putting a restraining order on me and trying to lock me up? What will it matter? My life will be over. Jesus, Chris, why did you have to get him involved? Why did you have to force me to do this? I was willing to be patient. I didn't like it, but I knew when that asshole Jonah went home you would have come back to me. I know it. We would have been together again. Why did you have to call the cops?"

Christian could not take his eyes off the gun resting against David's temple. Christian blinked hard, fast, but he could hold nothing inside any longer, and the wetness started to fall. "Please move the gun." Thickness lodged the words in Christian's throat, making them come out in a croak. "You don't have to put it down, but please...take it away from where it can hurt you."

David seemed like he stared at Christian's tears, but he suddenly jerked, shaking his head and jamming the gun deeper into the flesh at his temple. Christian cried out, and his heart stopped. The gun didn't go off, but Christian swayed, not sure how much more of this he could take.

"Please, David." Christian took a tentative step forward, his hands outstretched with his palms up. "Look at me." He made another small move and put them *almost* within touching distance. He kept his gaze locked to David's wary one. "Look at me, and remember the teasing guy who talked me out of my pants. I liked that guy so much. I know that David is inside you still, right now. I will help that man come to terms and figure out his new path; I promise you I will. But you have to put the gun down and take the first step."

David's hand shook, and his face weakened and fell. "Ok—No!" He kicked out with his leg and jammed Christian in the gut with his boot, careening him into the bed. "You won't trick me, Chris. You can't. It's over now." Christian heaved, trying to regain his breath and footing as he watched everything in David clear and become very calm. "You changed it all when you sicced that detective on me. You don't want to help me. You don't want anything to do with me. I heard you tell him to do whatever it takes to put me away. I can't have people find out. I can't go to jail." He cocked the weapon while looking right into Christian's eyes. "I'm sorry." His voice broke. "I can't."

Christian lunged off the bed and ran forward, screaming, "Nooo!" The door behind David exploded open at the same time, and Jonah appeared, charging too. Jonah tackled David just as Christian clipped the heel of his hand into David's elbow, dislodging his hold on the gun as it fired.

David cried a bloodcurdling wail as he hit the floor in a crush under Jonah, the sound so awful it shuddered right through Christian's body. Christian rolled to his knees, having fallen as well. Jonah quickly dug a knee into David's back and locked his hands there.

Christian looked up and found Jonah. The clear determination in Jonah's mercury eyes was the most beautiful thing Christian had ever seen. Christian choked on the swell of emotion, unable to contain it.

"Grab that sheet," Jonah said, jerking his head toward his bed. "Damn bastard didn't miss. He took a good chunk out of his scalp."

Processing Jonah's words, Christian moved fast, ripping back the plaid blanket to the blue sheet below. He yanked until the fabric released from its neat tuck and dragged it to a stop near David's head. He winced for David as he took in the gash that sliced through the upper part of his scalp. When Christian pressed the material against the wound to stanch the flow of blood, David didn't so much as flinch. Christian dipped down so he could see David's face and saw nothing but a vacant stare. David's chest rose and fell, though, so Christian knew he was alive.

"I think he has checked out," Jonah murmured, bringing Christian's focus back up to him. "At least for now."

"How about you?" Needing to touch, Christian reached out and caressed Jonah's cheek, jaw, mouth. There was still a solid man there his fingers could feel, and Christian almost started crying again. "He scared the shit out of me when he hit you. You were out cold, and there was blood."

"He underestimated my hard head." Jonah flashed a tight smile, but as he held Christian's gaze, his chin trembled. "Christ, it felt like it took me forever to get to the kitchen for a knife to cut the tape free. I didn't know what he would do to you or himself, and I didn't know if it was right to bust in, but I couldn't make myself stop. I had to get to you." He looked down at David, and Christian swore the temperature in the room dropped twenty degrees. "I could kill him right now." Jonah's voice was not at all steady anymore. "I could do it, Christian, and not even think twice."

Christian caressed Jonah's rough jaw and broke his stare on David. "No you couldn't." Christian said that with absolute confidence in his tone. "You can see him. He's fractured right now, and I don't even think he feels the wound he inflicted on himself." Christian glanced down, his heart hurting at the blank stare he found in David's eyes. Even so, he looked back up at Jonah, and the band tightened a thousand times harder around his chest at the uncertainty living in Jonah's eyes. "He's just a shell. He didn't want to hurt me; he wanted to hurt himself. You came in here and took him down to the ground, and never once did you think to deliver him additional pain."

"But if he'd hurt you—"

Christian ran his thumb along Jonah's lips, stopping that thought. "He didn't."

Right then, the sound of car tires screeched into asphalt, capturing Christian's full attention.

"That would be Braden," Jonah shared. "I dialed his number and just left the phone sitting there, figuring he would see our number and know something was up."

Our number. Shit.

A crash from the direction of the front of the house could only be the door being rammed open. "Christian!" Braden's voice boomed through the house. "Jonah! Fucking answer me!"

"In the second bedroom!" Christian shouted. "We're okay!" He connected his gaze to Jonah's once again. "Right?"

Braden appeared in the doorway, gun drawn, before Jonah answered. He took in the scene, holstered his weapon, and joined Jonah and Christian, kneeling next to David. "Shit. He moved fast." Quickly, Braden removed a pair of cuffs from the back of his pants, brushing Jonah's hold aside and locking the metal around David's wrists. Again, David didn't react.

That done, Braden fingered Jonah's neck, coming away with a trace of blood. He looked at the smear and then turned his attention down to David. Braden touched Christian's hand where it covered David's wound and moved it aside, pulling back the bunched-up sheet. He immediately pressed the material back down. "Damn it. I have EMTs and backup on the way." He waved a hand in front of David's eyes, and when he got no response, he looked to Christian and Jonah again. "What happened?"

Christian clenched his jaw. He tried to say the words, but his throat clamped tight once again. *Goddamnit, David.* He cleared the thickness away and forced himself to answer. "He tried to commit suicide."

Shifting, Braden gave Jonah his attention. "And you?" He pointed at Jonah's neck.

"He was in the house," Jonah answered. "Surprised us. He got me a couple of times in the back of the head and then locked himself and Christian in here."

Sirens cut through the quiet of the neighborhood, and soon the flash of red and blue lights streamed in through the windows, casting a strange hue across the men and room.

"That'll be the backup and EMTs." Braden's knees cracked as he stood. "Hang tight. I'll be right back."

Christian grabbed Braden's wrist before he took a step. "You'll stay with David's case through this process, right?" He knew he shouldn't care, but he couldn't abandon the friend he once knew. "Make sure he gets the help he needs?"

Braden nodded curtly. "I'll do what I can." Christian's hold fell away, and Braden pointed at Jonah's head as he passed. "When the guys come in, get that looked at. The paramedics are here for you too." He glanced at Christian. "That includes you. Don't let me hear you weren't tended to."

Jonah and Christian exchanged one last look, David on the floor between them, before all manner of men and women in various uniforms swamped the house and pulled them apart.

Chapter Fifteen

"Ohh, fuck..." Christian pressed his forehead against the shower wall as Jonah plunged into his ass from behind, ramming him deep. Jonah held Christian's hips in place with a rock-solid grip and pounded Christian's flaming channel with hard, fast strokes, fucking him with a frantic fury—as he had been doing since David's attack one week ago.

Hot water beat down on Jonah and Christian in a drumming thunder, and steam billowed in continuous clouds, making them both shiny and slick. Christian didn't know how Jonah managed to hold on, but he did, withdrawing his cock and then driving his length home again and again, making Christian gasp and grit his teeth. Nothing felt better than Jonah breaching his hole and filling his rectum; Christian welcomed it, even as he knew he would suffer soreness later. Jonah needed it, and Christian would give the man whatever he wanted.

Even if Jonah couldn't ask for whatever it was himself.

Christian curled his hand into a fist against the tile, digging his knuckles in as he reached down with his other hand and grabbed his own rigid dick. His cock jumped in his hand, every nerve ending inside shrieking for some of that same friction Jonah delivered to his ass.

As soon as Christian started to stroke himself, Jonah slid his hands up and wrapped them around Christian's chest, plastering their bodies together from top to bottom. Christian dropped his head back and leaned fully into Jonah's weight. Buried balls deep, Jonah breathed heavily next to Christian's ear as he looked over Christian's shoulder, down to his dick. "Christ, Christian, I love when you play with yourself." Jonah pumped with little pulses in Christian's ass, driving Christian's squeezing anus crazy with itching need for more. "Rub that cock hard." Christian pulled on his dick and fondled his balls in response, his breathing getting shallower with every new level of sensation. "More," Jonah said roughly, and Christian jerked harder, knowing how much Jonah loved it. "Oh yeah." Jonah started twisting and tugging on Christian's nipples. "Make yourself come."

Christian writhed his back against Jonah's front, reaching for that one last touch that would hurl him to release. "Uh-huh, uh-huh..." His testicles tingled, and his channel rippled with delight around Jonah's embedded length. "So good, Jonah. So"—Christian dragged his hand up and down his erection, handling the tip so roughly it hurt—"ahh...fucking good."

Jonah scraped his barely there nails across Christian's straining nipples, sank his teeth into Christian's neck, and delivered Christian straight to orgasm. Christian covered his slit with his palm, crying out as his entire body seized. His ass muscles clamped down on Jonah's invasion, and semen flowed in a long stream straight into Christian's hand. No sooner did warm spunk coat Christian's fingers than he lifted his hand to Jonah's mouth, offering his seed.

With the first lick across Christian's palm, Jonah whimpered and stilled. His cock swelled ridiculously in Christian's ass, stretching him unbearably, and he came. Wet heat filled Christian's sensitized tunnel, sending a shiver through him as he accepted the branding of Jonah's cum: wanted it, welcomed it, craved it, needed it…loved it.

As much as he loved the man.

Companionable silence filled the bathroom for a moment, relaxed bodies holding each other upright. Then Jonah straightened and withdrew, pausing only long enough to rub his fingers over Christian's hole, helping his ring settle back into place.

Christian shifted, glancing at Jonah, and caught him soaping up his cock.

Staring down at his now-flaccid dick, Jonah said, "Rodrigo is going to bang on the front door any minute now." Turning, Jonah stepped under the full stream of water and rinsed off. Quickly, he pulled back the shower curtain just enough to step over the rim. "We need to hurry it up. I'll go get us some coffee while you finish. Be back in a few."

By the time Christian yanked the curtain open the rest of the way, the bathroom was already empty.

This was Jonah's new MO. Get lost in sex and then run, hide, or claim exhaustion and fall asleep.

Today would be the final day of work on Mari's house, replacing the front porch. Since the incident with David, and Jonah's erratic behavior that had followed, Christian had no idea what to expect would happen when the renovations were complete.

He punched his fist into the wall.

Damn it.

* * *

Jonah pulled off his shirt and used it to wipe the back of his neck. Sweat ran in rivulets down his front and back, and he tried like hell not to stare at Christian, who had removed his T-shirt long ago. The day was nearly over, and with it, Jonah's reason for staying in Coleman. His excuse, really. He had a *reason*, and he damn well knew it.

Christian.

Jesus Christ, though. In the last seven days, every time Jonah paused for two seconds to think, his head filled with alternate endings to David's break-in, all of them concluding with bad, bad things befalling Christian. David could have shot Christian so easily, whether by accident or on purpose. David could have kidnapped Christian and taken him to a place where Jonah couldn't get to them in time. In his twisted need, David could have raped Christian or forced Christian to do things to him.

Jonah tried his best to act normally around Christian, but he couldn't stop the horrific images from crippling him, to the point where it sometimes physically hurt to even stand too close to Christian. Jonah found that he could hide the craziness in aggression and passion when they had sex, but as soon as the sexual haze faded, the panic crept back in, so debilitating that Jonah couldn't let Christian too close out of fear that Christian would see the ugliness of his thoughts.

David had scared Christian enough already, the man didn't need to deal with Jonah's imagination too.

A week ago, Jonah had pictured himself building a future with Christian—if Christian wanted one. This week changed everything. David's attack changed everything. Jonah could not do this...this being in a relationship thing. He'd spent his whole adult life wondering what in the hell was so broken in him that he couldn't *feel* things for other people, beyond the basics of common courtesy. Sometimes not even that. Before, he had hated being deficient when it seemed everyone around him was in love or falling there happily. Today, Jonah begged for that back. He wanted the numbness and could live with the confusion and loneliness, anything to take away this constant fear that ate at him more every day.

"Hello?" Christian's voice tore into the loop that played in Jonah's mind, spinning Jonah around, his muscles tightening, readying for an attack. Christian only had his cell phone to his ear, and Jonah slumped against the new porch, his legs shaking. Ever since David's break-in, Jonah had done the same damn thing every time something startled him; he jumped to level ten "find Christian and protect him" mode. Jonah barely slept, and other than leaving town, he didn't know how to make this awful feeling festering within him stop.

Christian held the phone to his ear for a long time without speaking. Jonah watched out of the corner of his eye, but Abby and Rodrigo didn't even pretend they weren't staring and trying to listen.

"Are you sure you have that information correct?" Christian finally said. And then, "Okay, thank you. We'll make an appointment and talk again soon. I appreciate the call. Good-bye."

Abby coiled her hair in her hand and fanned her neck. "Who was that?"

Christian didn't look to Abby; he pinpointed right in on Jonah from across the width of the porch. "That was the realtor."

Oh, shit.

Christian blinked, and this time his focus did shift to Abby. "Seems she was just busting at the seams and had to tell me we already have a very solid prospective buyer for the house."

From the porch, Abby reached down and squeezed Christian's shoulder. "That's so great."

"Yeah." Christian came back to Jonah, and he did not look happy. "One Mr. Jonah Roberts of Miami has made a very generous—and the realtor can now confirm—legitimate cash offer."

Jonah closed his eyes. *Shit shit shit.* He shook his head, faced Christian again, and did his best not to quake. "She should have been instructed by my realtor not to make the offer a formal one yet," he said. Jonah fought an internal battle to continue facing Christian when everything in him screamed that he could not have this talk right now. "Not until the house was officially completed, passed inspection, and was put on the market." *Not until I was gone.*

Clasping his hands behind his neck, Christian turned and paced a dozen feet away, stalled in the middle of the front yard for a drawn-out moment, and then came back to the porch. He slid his gaze to Rodrigo and Abby first. "Can you guys please excuse us?" He tunneled his fingers through his hair, scratching his head and mussing the thick locks along the way. "I don't know for how long. I'll call you when I'm ready for you to come back and help us finish the porch." He didn't wait for either to nod or say a word before he said, "Thank you."

Rodrigo swiped a couple of bottles of water out of a small cooler and beckoned to Abby with a jerk of his head. "Come on. You can come with me while I check in at a job site." He looked at a perspiring, dirty Abby before he yanked his T-shirt out of the waistband at the back of his jeans and put it back on. "We're not fit for anything else."

"Speak for yourself," Abby muttered. She did step carefully across the completed beams and down the steps, though. She raised a brow and chuckled. "Truth is, I might not even be fit for that."

Pausing by the driver's-side door of his truck, Rodrigo's gaze swept up and down the length of Abby's body. "You'll do," he said and climbed in behind the wheel.

Christian didn't even wait for Rodrigo's truck to leave the drive. He laid a piercing stare on Jonah that nicked Jonah's soul from ten feet away. "*You.*" The one word cut across the air sharply, cracking against Jonah's flesh. "Come with me. Right now." With nothing further, he moved with a purpose inside the house.

This was another deeper showing of the young man Jonah remembered, the quiet but confident teen who exuded certainty from deep within. A person who knew himself and his place in the world. Christian's energy—his very life force—pulled at Jonah, and he could not help but follow. Jonah stepped inside the house and found Christian pacing the width of the living room.

"Shut the door," Christian instructed, his voice harder than Jonah had ever heard it. "I know we've had audiences before, but this is not one for the neighbors' ears."

Jonah's heart raced, and he started sweating even more than he'd done outside. His hand shook, but he managed to do as Christian asked. Words couldn't get past the back part of his throat, though, so he just turned and made himself look at Christian when he finished.

Christian exploded. "What in the hell is going on with you? What are you trying to do or trying to pull or trying to achieve by putting in an offer on this house?" Christian swung around toward Jonah and stalked right up to where he stood. "Start talking to me, right now, or I swear to God I will throw a punch at you and damn well make it hurt. I don't care that I will break my hand doing it."

With his chest hurting and his throat constricting, Jonah prayed for divine intervention that would help him explain without breaking himself or frightening Christian. "You should live in this house, Christian," he said, his voice scratchy but audible. "You're supposed to. I could see it from the first night I got here fifteen years ago, and I could see it when I came back two and a half weeks ago. You belong here."

"So you just decided to buy it for me?" Christian snapped his fingers. "Just like that?"

"I can give it to you, and at the same time give Marisol's charities a big boost, as she requested." Jonah pursed his lips, so, so uncomfortable with this conversation. "I have the money. I don't go out and spend it; it just sits there." His entire body flamed with the heat of discomfort, and he thought he might burn anyone who touched him right now. "You know I don't like…doing public-type stuff. You know I'm not comfortable in most situations, so my money just sits there."

Christian tilted his head and studied Jonah, making him feel like a sideshow freak. "Uh-huh, and when did you do this?"

"D-do what?" *Jesus.* Jonah rubbed his palms on his jeans, trying to control the nervous perspiring.

Raising a brow, looking more cool and in control every minute they stood together, Christian asked, "When did you set this in motion? When did you contact your realtor and have her approach mine?"

Jonah clenched his teeth and bit off a terse curse. "A couple of days after I got here." *Why can't Christian just accept the house as a gift, as I intended it?* "You're at ease here, Christian. This place feeds you and makes you feel like you're home. I can see it in you; every day you spend here, you become more confident and more at peace with Marisol's death. I know you don't want to give it to some stranger. You don't want to turn it over to some person who won't feel the history in its very foundation the way you do."

"Agreed. You know me very well." Moving a few steps in, Christian stepped breathtakingly close to Jonah but didn't touch. Christian's *body* didn't make contact with Jonah's, anyway. Jonah felt like Christian reached through with his stare and touched the secrets hiding in Jonah's mind and heart. "Don't stop now," Christian said, his gaze penetrating Jonah's. "Keep talking, Jonah. There's more in there you want to say. Make yourself do it."

Something inside Jonah sparked, lighting the fuse of a bomb that Jonah knew he had to contain. He pivoted and wiggled like a worm, spinning himself out of Christian's proximity, something that he could not handle right now. "Goddamnit, Christian. What the hell do you want me to say?" His skin aching under the scrutiny, Jonah bolted for the new master bedroom. Ever since David locked himself in the other room with Christian, Jonah hadn't been able to sleep in there.

Fuck.

He whirled around and found Christian right on top of him. "Has this place changed for you?" He took a step backward, and his legs hit the edge of the bed. "Because of David? Is that why you're fighting taking the house?"

Christian shook his head. "David could never take away the love I feel when I'm in this place. Not even close." Christian's eyes remained steady, and Jonah knew he could never hope to reach the depths of Christian's inner strength. Or his peace. "Keep talking, Jonah. You're not where you want to go yet."

Jonah turned away and blinked, trying to contain the burn and pressure behind his eyes. Every second he stood this close to Christian, every minute he could feel Christian's body heat or listen to him speak, breached the dam Jonah had erected long ago to save his sanity. "I thought the place where I grew up was hell," he started roughly, unable to hold it in any longer. "When I told you that last week, it was the truth. But that feeling didn't even come close to what I felt, how scared I was, when David had you and I didn't know what he would do."

Christian's hands slid around Jonah's waist and went for the snap on his jeans. Jonah closed his eyes against the extra level of sensation, fighting with everything in him to deal adequately with one thing at a time. "Hell was every second it took to push my way to the kitchen and struggle to get a knife and cut that tape off my wrists and ankles. Hell was the ten seconds I wasted to call Braden, without knowing if that could be the difference between your life and death." Christian eased Jonah's jeans and underwear down to his thighs on the heels of those words. Jonah whimpered as his cock twitched with Christian's caress along his length. Right now, though, not even the promise of sex could break through the fear living inside Jonah, and he kept going. "Hell was making the decision to kick in that door. I was so scared I would just as easily set David off and bring about your death as rescue you."

Christian dropped to his knees behind Jonah and unlaced Jonah's boot. "You're still fighting it, baby." He pressed a kiss to Jonah's thigh, sending a shiver through Jonah. "Keep going."

Jonah lifted his leg on automatic so Christian could remove his boot and a moment later did the same for the other. Jonah felt stripped naked by Christian, in ways that struck so much deeper than the removal of his clothes. He felt knifed right up the middle and knew he should shut up right now, yet with Christian's every soft touch on his bare flesh and every murmur of encouragement that followed a light kiss to his ankle or back of his knee or hip, Jonah spoke words that he never thought to say. "I wanted it to be different with you, Christian. Christ, I promise I did. You're so wonderful, and I think I even felt happy for a short while, and I was starting to think that I wasn't a defect after all. But this week... Feeling the way I have since David..." Christian pecked kisses over each of Jonah's butt cheeks, and Jonah's legs started getting a little weak. Jonah shook his head and tried to regain order, but neither his mind nor his body obeyed. "I'm so scared, and all I can think about are the thousands of ways someone could hurt you, and I feel sick all the time because of it. When I used to look at other people and *want*, I didn't know it felt like this. I-I...I..." Like a scratch in a record that made it repeat the same spot, Jonah could not get another word past the clog in his throat. He exhaled through the lapse of control and looked straight ahead across the bed, to walls that he and Christian had painted, together. The future Jonah had so very secretly wished for from virtually the first day showing up on Marisol's door shouted at him in heart-wrenching wails, wringing a suffocating pain right through his core.

Jonah wanted to run from this place that hurt so much. He had to leave. He couldn't take this pain anymore.

Christian furrowed into Jonah's crack, *right then*, licking his ring, and took Jonah's legs right out from under him. Jonah's knees wobbled as raw, base sensation rocked through him. He fell face-first onto the bed, moaning directly into the mattress as Christian teased his tongue against Jonah's quivering sphincter once again. Fuck, Jonah had never felt anything like it. Christian took Jonah's ass in his hands and split his cheeks apart, then lapped right up and down the line of his crease, sending shiver after shiver through Jonah's body.

"Jesus—ahh—" Jonah pulled in a deep breath as Christian alternated between poking the tip of his tongue at Jonah's pucker and sucking the tight circle of muscle, making Jonah's toes curl over the edge of the bed. "Haven't"—he groaned as the image of Christian eating him filled his head—"haven't showered. Oh, damn...dirty, sweaty."

"Don't care," Christian murmured against Jonah's hole, pulsing vibrations over the nerve-rich area. Christian repeated probing and suckling on Jonah's entrance again, and Jonah bit into the comforter to keep from screaming. The blunt tip of something firmer, a finger or thumb, joined Christian's tongue at Jonah's asshole, applying a delicious pressure that had Jonah humping the bed as his cock grew painfully erect. His channel clenched repeatedly, already grabbing for something to fill the space that felt so empty without Christian inside him. Jonah hooked a hand around his left knee and pulled it up and to the side, spreading himself open even more, offering, begging without words, for Christian to take him.

Christian seemed to understand Jonah's need. He bore down on Jonah's ring and pushed through, taking Jonah's ass with his finger. Jonah let go of his leg and reached back, grabbing his ass cheek and splitting himself wide open.

"Please," he whispered, barely able to speak that one word.

Once again, Christian interpreted the rest of the sentence. He pulled out, spit, and eased two fingers inside, sliding to the second knuckle and tormenting Jonah's prostate. With every graze over that little bump of pleasure, Jonah's entire body buzzed with happy nerve endings that had never come to life before discovering Christian. Just when Jonah thought he couldn't take one more touch over his sweet spot without coming, Christian withdrew his fingers, leaving Jonah open and achingly bereft. His ring pulsed and started to settle, and then—then, *Holy Mother*— Christian licked all around Jonah again and thrust his tongue inside Jonah's ass.

Jonah's backside shot up and off the bed, smashing into Christian's face as he struggled to accept this insanely intimate level of fucking. Christian dug his fingers into Jonah's hips and held him in place; he snaked his tongue in and out of Jonah's chute, driving Jonah wild. Jonah's cock strained and leaked, jamming into the mattress, and even his nipples stood at attention all on their own, abrading against the bedding and making him nuts with every scrape.

The fuse inside Jonah that had been lit a moment ago— or perhaps it went all the way back to when they were teenagers—was only moments away from detonating. Jonah looked back at Christian, saw Christian's face tucked in the hills of his ass, but somehow found Christian's dark gaze, full of light. Christian was already naked too, and Jonah could barely think to wonder how far gone he'd been that he hadn't even noticed Christian pause to take off his clothes. He was just damned glad they were already on the floor.

"Fuck me, Christian." Jonah didn't know if he asked, ordered, pleaded, or begged; he just knew it was guttural and full of need. "I want to feel you all the way inside me right now."

Christian nodded, spit into Jonah's entrance some more, and pressed a final kiss to Jonah's fluttering hole. He then licked a continuous line from that point all the way up the indent of Jonah's spine to his neck and right to Jonah's ear. "Roll over." Christian lifted into a push-up stance, and Jonah shifted onto his back, settling with spread legs. "We're not nearly done yet." Christian drizzled spit into his hand and rubbed it over his cock before nudging the tip against Jonah's entrance. "Say what you really want to say." Christian looked into Jonah's eyes and easily held him prisoner with nothing more than that. "Tell me why you want to buy this house." Christian entwined his fingers with Jonah's, pressed the backs of them into the mattress, and without blinking, took Jonah's ass, pushing his cock home.

Jonah couldn't look away, and he welcomed the stretch and immediate, sharp burn that took over his sphincter and rectum as Christian invaded him with nothing more than saliva. Jonah only grew more excited, and his balls and cock responded to the elemental coupling by tightening immeasurably, making him gasp. Christian sat lodged, big and unmoving, inside Jonah's channel, his gaze not leaving Jonah's, and pushed Jonah near to insanity. Jonah tried to thrust up with his hips and get them going, but it was as if

Christian's pinned Jonah to the bed with the piercing of his cock. Even with his superior build, Jonah could not move.

Christian dipped down and brushed his lips against Jonah's, and gave him a hint of tongue. He drew back before Jonah could grab for more and once again looked into Jonah's eyes. "Tell me, baby. Tell me why you want this house."

Jonah blinked hard and stared up into Christian's beautiful, confident eyes, almost unable to breathe with the pressure that bore down on his chest, suffocating him. "I want to live here." Moisture leaked down to his temple, a hard-fought tear mingling with the sweat. "Together. With you."

Lowering his lips again, this time Christian sipped from the wetness streaming down Jonah's temple into his hair. "Why?" He pushed the word right into Jonah's ear.

With no control over his hands, Jonah wrapped his legs around Christian's waist, holding him in another way. Christ, he needed this man and could not bury it anymore. "When I'm with you, I feel connected to the world and the way I think a normal person is supposed to feel. I feel like I matter to you."

Christian rubbed his lips across Jonah's cheeks, and forehead, nose, *connecting.* The light touches felt so damn loving Jonah couldn't hide anything or shut up. "But I'm scared shitless that I'm going to lose you, and I can't stop these terrible pictures from crippling me." He turned his head, found Christian's mouth, and captured it in a kiss to stifle a sob. He kissed Christian with every desperate feeling in him, and he swore Christian absorbed every bit of it and gave him strength in return. The kiss grew deeper and more frantic, and with it, Christian started to move, digging slow thrusts into Jonah's ass with his embedded cock. Jonah gasped with a mixture of pain and pleasure, and Christian took the opportunity to sink his tongue deep inside Jonah's mouth, mimicking every slide of his shaft into Jonah's channel below.

Jonah's dick jammed into Christian's belly with every shove down, and after a few pokes, Christian released one of Jonah's hands and dived between their stomachs, taking Jonah's prick in his fist. Christian squeezed Jonah's length and pulled up from the base, making Jonah's passage ripple around Christian's cock in kind. In response, Jonah grabbed Christian's upper arm and started thrusting upward with every push downward from Christian. He clamped his fingers on Christian's hard biceps with each slide of hand on his erection or thrust in his ass. Christian had a beautiful body, and it could do such amazing things to Jonah that he whimpered with overwhelming feeling, both physical and emotional.

Christian bit at Jonah's kiss-swollen lips and looked into his eyes. "Finish it, Jonah," he said, his voice as strong as the pounding and jerking he continued to deliver to Jonah's body. "You're not there yet."

Jonah slid his hand up Christian's arm and clung to Christian's neck, keeping their lips nearly touching and their gazes so close everything was a blur. "I'm scared to stay here in Coleman." The raw confession ripped through him in a rough wave, tearing up his clogged throat. "But I don't want to go. I don't want to leave you." He pressed his lips to

Christian's and squeezed his eyes shut. "I love you, Christian. Please don't let me run."

Gentle fingers wiped the corners of his eyes. "You're not going anywhere, baby." Christian teased the tip of his tongue through Jonah's lips. "I love you too," he confessed, sending the words directly into Jonah's mouth and down into his soul. "I promise."

Jonah's eyes popped open, and he found Christian waiting for him there, patient and with a soft smile. Christian nodded. "I swear."

"Yeah?"

Christian grazed Jonah's face with the tips of his fingers. "Yeah."

No movement. With Christian's body as still as Jonah's, and nothing more than words and a stare, both men came. Christian's hot seed filled Jonah's ass, warming his walls at the same time Jonah released on Christian's stomach, splashing him with thick lines of cum. Their bodies pulsed in tandem, and their breathing became one as well.

After a long moment of silence that hung suspended in the air, Christian exhaled and shifted to his side, taking Jonah with him. Still buried inside Jonah, Christian soothed the small of Jonah's back with one hand and brushed the back of his other across Jonah's cheek and into his hair. Christian looked at Jonah, offered a soft smile, and Jonah lost his heart all over again.

"I've been scared to push you to talk to me," Christian started. He continued to pet at Jonah as he did. "You set me off today, though. I prayed I wasn't going to lose you over it, but I couldn't hold back anymore, and I couldn't let you do it either. Not if it meant you leaving."

Jonah captured Christian's hand and trapped it against his heart, letting him feel the beating there that existed for Christian. "How did you know?" *That I love you, when I hadn't even said the words to myself.* Jonah opened his mouth, but nothing more came out.

Christian's gaze softened, and once again, it was as if he could see Jonah's thoughts that he didn't yet know how to fully express. "When you said you'd put in motion buying the house over a week ago, I trusted that I knew how you felt then, even though you'd pulled way back with me since." Christian dipped down and pressed a kiss to Jonah's hand. "I had to take a chance. I didn't want you to leave."

"I didn't want to go." It was rusty, and the words still scraped when they came out, but Jonah forced himself to find them and give them to Christian. "I don't know anything about these things I'm feeling or how I can be sure about them or how I can trust that it's real when it happened so fast, but I know I love you and that it's right." Jonah reached between them and rubbed the tattoo on his belly. Under the stickiness of seed, he swore it burned hot with approval.

Following Jonah's hand with his, Christian stroked over the tattoo Jonah fingered. "Tell me about that one," he requested. "With the meaning the one on your shoulder has, I know this one must hold something important for you too."

Jonah rolled onto his back, and with it, finally separated his body from Christian's. Christian sat up and crossed his legs, and Jonah put one hand on Christian's thigh, needing the connection. With the other, he traced the key in the center of the design. "The key I had done when I took ownership of the first bike shop. It represents the key to my future, as well as a literal key to the business. A man named Henry owned the shop. He mentored me while I was in JD and gave me a job when I was released. He helped keep me on the right path and he sold me the place when he retired." Jonah looked down as he fingered the darkly shaded wing that curled like one half of yin and yang. "This is an angel wing that represents Henry. I got it when he died a few years ago." Jonah put his hand on the other wing and swore he could still feel it being inked into his flesh. "This wing I got three weeks ago, right after I got word of Marisol's death. I realized that even though I never saw her again after I moved to Miami, she was as big a part of changing my life as Henry was, and she deserved a place right next to Henry."

"You have a poet's soul, and you don't even know it."

Jonah chuckled, a little uncomfortable with such praise. "I don't know about that."

"What about your businesses?" Christian's smile stalled midway. "If you really do want to live in this house with me..."

"I do." Jonah shot up and cuffed his hand around Christian's neck, pulling him close. "I'll work all that out. I have someone in charge right now that I trust, and maybe I can see if he's interested in a permanent promotion. I don't want to sell the shops; there are too many guys there who need a second chance, like I did, and I'd be afraid someone new might let them go. Miami is not that bad a drive. I could go down there on a regular basis and make sure things are working the way I want them to." Jonah felt his cheeks reddening, but now that he had found this acceptance in Christian, he couldn't seem to stop. "I could maybe even look into buying a building here and opening a new shop, perhaps tie it into Marisol's life work and make some money for her charities while I'm at it."

Christian smiled and smacked a kiss on Jonah's lips. He quirked his head to the side. "You've been thinking about this for a lot longer than the last five minutes, haven't you?" His eyes danced with pure light, arresting Jonah's heart.

Jonah sensed he should tease back, but when his gaze held Christian's, only complete truth came out. "I started seeing a different future the second I laid eyes on you again, but I was so scared to hope." He rose up on his knees and brought Christian with him, tilting his face up and touching their lips. "I never forgot you, Christian. Not in all these years. I just never dared dream we could end up together like this."

Christian slanted his lips across Jonah's and took his mouth with a hard, fast kiss, delivering a promise before pulling away. "You never left me either, and I know now that we're going to figure everything out and be okay." Christian held Jonah's face, and in his touch, Jonah could feel his strength and conviction. Then Christian smiled and lit up Jonah's soul. "But how about for today, we shower and finish our new porch?" Christian bounced off the bed, full of energy and life. Standing naked, his hand outstretched, he looked more stunning than was fair. "Sound good to you?"

Our new porch. Those words resonated deeply, racing right to Jonah's heart.

"Are you coming, baby?" Christian shook his outstretched hand in Jonah's direction.

Yeah.

"Absolutely." Thinking about what he could do with the man he loved while having that shower, Jonah linked his hand in Christian's, absorbed his warmth, and happily followed.

Epilogue

"Where are we going?" Christian shouted so Jonah could hear him over the roar of the motorcycle. Christian had his arms wrapped around Jonah's hard waist, his chest fused to Jonah's back, and his chin planted firmly on Jonah's shoulder. "I want you naked in our bed. I missed you."

"Soon." Jonah let go with one hand for a moment and covered Christian's grip on his stomach, squeezing firmly. "Hold on!"

Jonah let go of Christian and put the motorcycle into a turn, tilting them precariously in a way that still set off the butterflies in Christian's stomach. He knew they would be fine, and a rush of adrenaline always shot through him after Jonah took him for a drive, but Christian's heart still raced like mad every time he got on the back of Jonah's Harley.

Giving up on getting any information out of Jonah—at least for the moment—Christian snuggled into his partner's body from behind and inhaled, letting Jonah's natural musk seep into his pores. God, Jonah had been down in Miami for two weeks tending to business, and Christian could not believe how much trouble he had sleeping without Jonah sharing their bed. Three months into living together and having someone he loved to come home to every night had

Christian spoiled for a big, warm body in the house with him. Consequently, he did a lot of butting into his friends' lives on the days when Jonah was away.

Christian chuckled. Last night Abby had called Christian cute but pathetic, but then admitted she envied the bond Jonah and Christian shared. She got a wistful look in her eyes as she said it, and Christian wondered if she thought about Rodrigo or maybe even Braden Crenshaw at that moment. Christian had a feeling she could have either man if she would just admit that she wanted something more than the single life she swore she embraced.

Jonah suddenly veered the motorcycle off the busier road they traveled and took them about a half mile down a district of industrial buildings and warehouses. He turned again, into an empty parking lot, and eased the bike to a stop. Jonah kicked the stand out, climbed off, and removed his helmet, revealing his mess of hair and handsome face.

Setting his helmet down on the seat, he pulled Christian's headgear off and put that down too. Jonah ran his palm up Christian's cheek and dug his fingers into Christian's hair, pulling him close. "I missed you too, by the way," he said softly, his pale gaze intense but loving. He scraped his mouth across Christian's, letting their lips cling together for an extended moment. "Sorry I dragged you onto the bike right when I got home and didn't give you a better hello."

Christian rubbed his hands up and down Jonah's chest, letting the feel of his amazing body become familiar again. Christian's cock immediately responded, but he reluctantly let his hands drop to his sides. "You can make up for it later." He couldn't resist one more quick peck to Jonah's cheek before climbing off the bike himself. "So, what is this?" He looked around. "Why are we here?"

"This"—Jonah waved his arm toward the huge brick warehouse—"is my new bike shop. Well, it will be, once I get the necessary equipment installed and hire some guys— or girls. I have a few women working for me down south. Come on." Jonah grabbed Christian's hand and dragged him toward the warehouse. "Let me show you the inside. This truly is a gutted building, so I can create what I want from scratch. That will help everything move very fast."

They walked around the side of the building. When they got to a metal door, Christian leaned his shoulder into the wall, waiting for Jonah to unlock the door and let them inside. Christian stared openly, his chest filling with pride and love at the confidence he saw in the man before him. This—his business—was Jonah's strength, and it was fucking sexy.

Christian reached out and ran his hand up Jonah's arm to his shoulder, his palm still tingling and burning with the slightest skin-on-skin contact, even if he knew it wouldn't lead to anything more…at least not at the moment.

Jonah turned to Christian, pausing in the middle of pushing open the door. "What?"

Shrugging as he pushed away from the wall, Christian said, "Nothing, really. I can just see how excited you are; that's all. It makes me proud." As Christian slid past Jonah to get inside the building, he made sure to get very, very close. He looked up into Jonah's eyes as the bulges in their jeans briefly grazed one another. "And horny." Christian walked inside the building, knowing well by now that Jonah stared right at his ass.

Jonah quickly moved in behind and pulled Christian to his front, rubbing his cock against Christian's backside. He leaned down and whispered in Christian's ear, "Keep teasing me with that little wiggle and you'll end up facedown on this dirty floor with my dick rammed all the way up your ass."

Goddamn. Christian groaned and had his hands on his belt in two seconds flat. Cursing his lapse of control, he stamped down his need and pulled away. Turning, he scanned the huge open space, taking deep breaths until he was steady enough to face Jonah again. "Maybe we'll get to that later." Christian started strolling the perimeter, moving in and out of beams of light streaming in through dirty windows that sat high on the walls. "Tell me why you rushed me here the moment you got home." He looked at Jonah from across the width of the area. "Tell me about this place."

"This is how you'll believe I'm truly settled here in Coleman," Jonah said. He held Christian to him with his eyes. "Building this new place from the ground up will be my priority. I've never done that before, and I think it will be a great new challenge. While I was down south these past few weeks, I talked with Cam and formally put him in charge of overseeing the shops down there. I also talked to a couple of guys who've earned the right to help manage the shop where they each work. It's taken care of; promotions, raises, paperwork, and contracts have been signed to make it all official."

Both men circled the building, looking at each other. They moved in, getting a bit closer with each turn around the floor.

"I've had my eye on this place," Jonah said, "but I didn't want to show it to you until I knew I could do it without worrying about my places in Miami. I'm committed to this town with a business now, as well as my tie to you. I know you never said it out loud, but I could see in your eyes that you worried if I'd last here without something of my own."

Christian's breathing grew heavier, and something in him felt strung tight, as if a coil would soon snap. "Not so much that you would leave," he said, "just that you wouldn't be satisfied without doing something you so clearly love."

Jonah nodded, and his nostrils flared. "Seeing this place and getting a better sense of my plans"—Jonah sounded breathy too—"I hope you won't worry about that anymore."

They were within a mere half dozen feet of each other now, yet they still moved in a circle. "I won't."

"Good." Jonah nodded. His hands curled into fists at his sides; then the fingers opened and spread, only to close again. "I did something else while I was in Miami. Something"— Jonah came to a stop within touching distance, and Christian followed suit—"I need you to see."

"Oh?" No alarm bell sounded in Christian at all. He knew Jonah would never hurt him. "What's that?"

Jonah stared at Christian so intently he felt penetrated as deeply as when they made love. Then, Jonah turned, shrugged up his T-shirt, and pulled it over his head. Once it cleared him, he tucked the hem into the back of his pants.

Christian gasped, and his hand flew to his mouth. Tears filled his eyes as he looked, already knowing deep in his soul what he saw.

Jonah turned and faced Christian once more. "This is you, Christian." He touched the new tattoo on his formerly bare shoulder—*a second wing.* It was a simple, beautiful match to the first. Jonah's voice had never sounded so raw and vulnerable, and his big body had never trembled so much. "You are the other half of my freedom. I believe I can fly now because I have you."

His heart bursting for this man, Christian flew into Jonah's arms, knowing Jonah would always catch him. Jonah cried out and lifted Christian up, bruising him in a suffocating hold around his waist and back. Christian didn't care. He wrapped his arms around Jonah's neck and twined his legs around Jonah's waist, and squeezed him back just as tightly.

Christian kissed Jonah's shoulder, all over the inked flesh, then ran kiss after kiss up his neck to his ear. "I love you," he said, his own voice as rough as Jonah's had been moments ago. "You are strong and brave and beautiful, and it is my honor to know you and be loved by you." Christian kissed his way down Jonah's cut jaw and over his chin, to finally claim his mouth. Their tongues brushed softly at first, then tangled with bites and moans in between. Christian ached for more, and he finally had his man home to make it better. He pulled his head back and found Jonah's gaze shot with silver. Rubbing at the edge of Jonah's wide mouth, Christian smiled and said, "Take me home so that I can kiss every inch of you at my leisure. I will have you screaming to come before I finally roll over and beg you to fill me with every damn inch of your wonderful cock."

Jonah's fingers curled and dug into Christian's back. "Christ, I missed you. I like the sound of that." Jonah walked them toward the door, Christian still in his arms, all the while mixing searching kisses with sure words of love.

 **THE END**

Cameron Dane

I am an air force brat and spent most of my growing up years living overseas in Italy and England, as well as Florida, Georgia, Ohio, and Virginia while we were stateside. I now live in Florida once again with my big, wonderfully pushy family and my three-legged cat, Harry. I have been reading romance novels since I was twelve years old, and twenty years later I still adore them. Currently, I have an unexplainable obsession with hockey goaltenders, and an unabashed affection for *The Daily Show* with Jon Stewart.

I'd love to hear from you! Visit me on the Web at http://www.camerondane.com.

TITLES AVAILABLE In Print from Loose Id®

ALTERED HEART
Kate Steele

CROSSING BORDERS
Z. A. Maxfield

FAITH & FIDELITY
Tere Michaels

FORGOTTEN SONG
Ally Blue

HEAVEN SENT: HELL & PURGATORY
Jet Mykles

HEAVEN SENT 2
Jet Mykles

LOVERS, DREAMERS, AND ME
Willa Okati

RUSH IN THE DARK: COMMON POWERS 2
Lynn Lorenz

SLAVE BOY

Evangeline Anderson

SOUL BONDS: COMMON POWERS 1

Lynn Lorenz

ST. NACHO'S

Z. A. Maxfield

THE ASSIGNMENT

Evangeline Anderson

THE BITE BEFORE CHRISTMAS

Laura Baumbach, Sedonia Guillone, and Kit Tunstall

THE BROKEN H

J. L. Langley

THE TIN STAR

J. L. Langley

CPSIA information can be obtained at www.ICGtesting.com
Printed in the USA
BVOW012155061112

304834BV00001B/35/P

9 781607 374015